ICE DOGS

ICE DOGS

by

Terry Lynn Johnson

Houghton Mifflin Harcourt

Boston   New York

www.hmhco.com

The text of this book is set in Bembo.

The Library of Congress has cataloged the hardcover edition as follows:
Johnson, Terry Lynn.
Ice dogs/by Terry Lynn Johnson.
p. cm.
Summary: In this survival story set in Alaska, fourteen-year-old Vicky and
her dog sled team find an injured sledder in the wilderness.
[1. Dogsledding—Fiction. 2. Sled dogs—Fiction. 3. Dogs—Fiction.
4. Survival—Fiction. 5. Wilderness areas—Fiction. 6. Alaska—Fiction.]
I. Title.
PZ7.J63835Ic2013
[Fic]—dc23
2012045061

ISBN: 978-0-547-89926-8 hardcover
ISBN: 978-0-544-66387-9 paperback

Manufactured in the United States of America
DOC 10 9 8 7 6 5 4 3 2 1

4500562612

For my parents.
Both are long-suffering but supportive fans
of all my ill-advised adventures.

1

SATURDAY

ALL EIGHT OF MY DOGS ARE stretched in front of me in pairs along the gangline. They claw the ground in frustration as the loudspeaker blares.

"Here's team number five. Our hometown girl, fourteen-year-old Victoria Secord!"

A male voice booms out my racing stats while my lead dog, Bean, whips his crooked rat tail. He tries to lunge forward, and then catches my eye and screams with a pitch that shoots up my spinal cord and electrifies my teeth.

"Easy!" I grip the sled with shaking hands. I freaking *hate* starts.

With close to a hundred dogs here, the energy in the air is frantic. The bawling of the dogs in the team behind me echoes in my ears while the distinct odor of dog doo smeared under my runners assaults my nose. I try to focus on my dogs and the race chute ahead. Not the burning need to win. Not the fact that there's no one here to cheer for me.

"We gotcha." Two burly guys kneeling on the start line struggle to hold my bucking sled stanchions.

"Three, two, one, GO!"

We leap forward and shoot through Wicker's parking lot. The main race sponsor insisted we start at his feed store, even though it's three blocks away from the trailhead. They trucked in snow to get us through the streets, but as we skid through the dirty slush, I can tell this is a bad idea. Mushers need a real snow base for any kind of control.

My frozen eyelashes stick together, and I swipe at them as I peer ahead. We fly to the first corner, my heart pounding.

"Haw!" I shout.

My leaders swerve left, and the dogsled skids sideways. We're gaining momentum. With the wind cutting into my face, it feels as if I'm being sling-shot out of a jet.

A red Chevette is the last in a line of parked vehicles along the other side of the road. I crouch lower, stick my left foot out, and dig the heel of my mukluk in to carve a tighter turn.

The sled continues skidding—closer, closer.

I jump on the brake, smashing the two metal points into the ground with every ounce of my five-foot-nothing frame. Still we skid. And then we careen into the door, my teeth rattling with the impact. A metal screech announces the collision to everyone. I hear a grinding pop.

We clear the car, and I look down to see a little extra weight in the sled bag—a side mirror. Glancing around to see if anyone noticed, I grab it and nonchalantly toss it away. The cold wind whistles through me when I grin.

I turn my attention back to my dogs. My leaders, Bean and Blue, dig for the trailhead with matching strides. Blue's classic husky coat, with his black and white facemask, is even more striking next to Bean's rusty-propane-tank shade of fur.

We hurtle down the middle of the street that's been blocked off for the race. Now that they're running, my dogs are all business, focused ahead with tight tuglines. My heart squeezes with pride. They don't glance up as they barrel past a crouched photographer with a telephoto lens. They even ignore the smell coming from the hot dog stand next to the coffee shop. We catapult past a truck with its doors open blasting country music, past the historic log building that is the trading post with the two moose over the door. Someone had found the two sets of antlers locked together and the scene of how the animals died is forever replicated. When I was young, I could hardly stand to look at it, imagining what the moose had to endure, stuck together in battle, helpless and starving to death in the bush.

Finally we're past Main Street, and we slip by the snow fencing that funnels us toward the trail.

I feel an instant calm.

The din of the crowd fades behind us. It's just me and the dogs and the sunbeams breaking through the spruce branches stretching across the trail like cold fingers. The runners slice over the snow making their familiar *shhhh* sounds. I breathe in the tang of spruce pitch and the icy air is sharp in my throat.

But the most important thing is the dogs. It's always about the dogs.

I watch the way Whistler paces with her lopsided gait, the way Bean flicks his ears back to check on me, and how they all run together as if listening to the same beat of a drum, like a dragon boat team paddling in sync.

Bean and I have some kind of soul connection that I can't explain. I have a connection with all of my dogs, but Bean just gets me. I like to imagine we were friends in another life. Not that I believe in that, but there's no other way to describe that day when he was a pup and we looked at each other. Recognition. It's Bean who I greet first in the dog yard every morning, or when I get home from school. We have conversations. Sarah Charlie calls it crazy. She worries that I've changed too much since the accident.

"It's not healthy to just want to be with your dogs, Vicky. Life is about more than racing. You need to try to get back in the game. Remember when we used to have *fun*?"

I shake my head and lightly touch my good

luck mink. It's a narrow pewter charm as long as my hand that's hung around the handlebar of my dogsled since Dad gave it to me when I was nine. I've secretly named it Mr. Minky.

I pat the base of my nose with a shaky mitt, and call to the dogs. "Good dog, Blue, attaboy! Easy, Dorset. Who's a good girl?"

Their ears swivel back, but they keep trotting ahead. The sled bumps and skips over dips in the hard-packed trail. I pedal my foot to help the dogs pull faster. I want to win this race for Dad. I glance at Mr. Minky, and then concentrate on the trail.

As the dogs take a corner, I lean out from the handlebar. We skid, snow spraying out from the runners. Tears squeeze out the corners of my eyes and freeze in lines across my temples. I blink rapidly to stop my eyelashes from sticking together again.

Some mushers wear ski goggles, but I don't like how looking through goggles separates me from my environment. I like to see things clearly.

The dogs have good speed coming out of the turn. They're really pulling, as if they know we need to win. But they should drop back to their trots—we have a long way to go yet.

"Easy. Easy, dogs."

They run faster, smoking around a poplar stand. When we get to a straight stretch I look ahead. And then I see the wolf.

2.

THE WOLF IS A BEAUTIFUL, burnished brown loner. Or he seems to be, as I can't see any others around. He's a big one too, about a hundred pounds. He's trotting right along the trail. The dogs speed up even more, and I can feel the power come up through my feet and into the handlebar. We're running so fast, the wind cuts into my cheeks. I hunch forward and squint.

We're gaining on the wolf, even though he's loping now, and I'm torn between excitement and worry. Alaskan wolves don't normally get along with pets. Sled dogs are probably tougher than the average pet, but since they're about half the weight of a healthy wolf, they'd still be ripped apart. A few years ago dogs and cats started going missing in town. A bounty was put on the wolves and many of them were shot. I didn't like that, but I don't want any of my dogs to be snacks.

We're less than two team-lengths away when the wolf suddenly stops. Just stops dead on the trail. He turns around and stares at us. Bean and Blue slam on the brakes and do a move that looks as if they're tucking under the snow while doing a backwards somersault. All the dogs behind them pile up before I can slam my own brake. Then I throw down the snow hook and stomp on it.

When I look up at the wolf, our eyes meet and hold. He stands like royalty and stares directly into my soul.

Assessing me.

I'm enveloped and frozen in his spell. He's gorgeous. Wild.

My breath catches like a hiccup in my throat. I glance at the dogs and the moment is gone.

"Hey, wolf. Git!" I do a false charge toward him.

He spins and trots in a beeline toward the trees. Not in a frightened way, but with dignity. He leaves a path of silence except for the pounding in my ears. For a few breaths, the dogs are absolutely still. They stand in a tangled mess all sheepish-looking. Then they begin to squirm and mutter to each other. Bean shoots me a look with eyes as big as panic buttons.

"Yeah, that's what you get for chasing a wolf, Bean Brain. What did you think was going to happen?" I grab the tuglines of the two leaders and walk backwards along the trail to stretch out the team. Whistler's tugline is wrapped around her back leg. When she feels it pinch her as it tightens, she growls at Gazoo.

"Hey! Enough." I sort out tuglines, necklines,

unclip a few dogs, straighten them out, then clip them back in. My legs still feel shaky.

The dogs start to whine, and Drift screams and slams on her tug to get running. Dorset leaps on her and they exchange savage growls and shrieks — teeth flashing, whites of their eyes showing. In the next instant, that conversation is over and they go back to barking at the trail ahead. I wish I could be more like that. Just lay into someone who's bugging me. Well, I guess I don't have much trouble with that part. But once I've said it, I'd like to just let it go.

Drift succeeds in popping the snow hook, but I grab the sled as it goes by and swing onto the runners.

"All right, Beanie. Let's go. That a boy!"

Uncle Leonard should be heading to the finish line by now. Sarah wonders how I can stand having Uncle Leonard around since he looks so much like my dad, but I don't think he looks that much like him. I look more like Dad, with my tan complexion and thick dark hair that cowlicks right in the front of my forehead. Dad had a habit of slowly running his hands through his hair when he was deep in thought, so his hair usually stood straight up. He was a methodical thinker.

Unfortunately, I don't think that trait rubbed off on me, but I definitely inherited his dog-training talent.

"Dad," I whisper.

Bean glances over his shoulder at me. I wipe my nose and straighten my shoulders.

After another hour of running, I can tell by the way the dogs' ears perk forward and their increased speed that there's something ahead. They smell and hear things way before I do. I wish I had senses like that. But being with them means I do have those senses. I read my dogs constantly to be aware of their moods and what they're telling me.

A tangle of alders shields my view until we skid around the corner and I see two teams far in front of us. From this distance, the orange of the mushers' race bibs stands out against the snow fencing as they glide toward the crowds. They cross the finish line to muted cheering. Since this is a timed race, I won't know till later how well we did, but I'm pretty sure we should've passed those two teams to be in the running. The wolf has cost us time. The dogs' ears twitch back when I groan with frustration.

It takes us several more minutes to run the home stretch and trot through.

"Vicky! Over here." Uncle Leonard strides forward on long legs covered with tan Carhartt overalls. The overalls and his lined canvas Carhartt jacket are pretty much the only things I ever see him wear. Even in summer. The rest of the guys he works with all wear the same. A couple of times I've gone by the construction sites and it looked like an episode of *Deadliest Catch*, minus the rubbers.

"Hey, kiddo, great race! Did you have fun?" Uncle Leonard grabs my leaders with a bare hand, and steers them toward the dog truck.

"Yeah, but we couldn't catch Cook and that other team. Who's the other one, anyway?"

A bucket full of bloody, chicken-laced water sits on the ground near the back tire and the first four dogs all try to stick their heads in at once.

"I dunno, but that Cook has himself some fast dogs."

"Git! Out of there, wait your turn." I wrestle the dogs over to the drop lines attached to the truck and clip one to Bean's tug to keep the line straight.

If our time puts us in the top ten, we qualify for the White Wolf Classic. Imagining Dad's pride if he knew I made it to the White Wolf this year fills me with a yearning so thick, I can taste it. The need to win has been the most important thing in my life this winter.

I grab the bowls off the tailgate and toss one to each dog down the gangline. "We're going to make it to White Wolf, right, Uncle Leonard?"

"You bet, kiddo." Uncle Leonard leans toward me, his face all graying whiskers and tanned squint lines.

"I heard some interesting rumors while I was waiting," he says, in a gruff attempt at whispering. "Seems Cook lost his job at the mill. May be getting out of dogs." He gives me a pointed look with his brown eyes peeking out below his fur hat.

I glance over at Cook's truck with all his champions bent over drinking. Out of dogs? I've run with Cook on our trails at home. I can't believe he'd be getting out of dogs. He loves his dogs.

Drift rakes her front claws down my shin and stares up at me.

"Sorry, girl. I'm getting it."

I stir the bucket with the long-handled scoop. Bits of pulpy chicken gobs float around in the red liquid. We bait the water in winter to get the dogs to drink it before it freezes. The only problem is that it spoils them and they get fussy drinking plain water.

I start at the leaders and scoop the raw-smelling water into their bowls, then continue down the line. Drift bounces up and down. Whistler dumps her bowl over to eat the chunks off the snow.

"Picky girl." I'm pouring more water in it when Drift suddenly scuttles sideways under her partner, Dorset, as far away as her neckline reaches.

I turn to see a man approaching wearing a puffy, light green parka. As he marches closer, he takes off his fancy North Face glove and holds out his hand. His face is red with a flat nose. Surrounded by the thick coat, he looks like a stuffed olive.

"Russell Price from Endurance Dog Food," he says.

"Um. Victoria from Secord Kennels." I take his hand, but remember too late I still have on my dirty fingerless gloves.

"Yes, indeed. Harold Wicker tells me you're quite the racer. Says your dogs eat Endurance from his store."

"Yeah. My dogs like it." My voice sounds small

17

and far away as blood charges through my veins. Why did he come to talk to me? Is he checking out my team for future reference? Maybe as a contender for the White Wolf?

"Your team does quite well in the racing circuit. And you run the kennel yourself, I understand?"

"Yes, I run and train them myself. I think we do well since I'm a lot smaller than most of the mushers here — less weight for my dogs to pull." There's a short silence that I rush to fill. "Well, I'm small for my age. I'm almost fifteen. Anyway. My size is good for dogsledding — not so great when I try to find clothes without Disney princesses all over them." I'm horrified to hear some kind of gargled giggle come out of me, and my face heats up.

Russell scratches his nose and scans the dogs. He looks over at the dog truck and the sled. The pause in our conversation feels thick with significance. Thankfully, the slurping of the dogs licking their bowls clean covers it. Gazoo and Whistler have a short scrap over whose bowl is whose. While Drift is busy watching us, her partner leans over and steals her bowl by dragging it with her teeth.

"Well, congratulations on your smart finish. Guess you'll have to wait for a while yet to know your results. But very impressive. I wish you well."

I watch him walk over to Cook's team next, and I kneel down to bury my face in Gazoo's neck ruff.

"I wonder what brings the Endurance food rep out to this race," Uncle Leonard says. "Think he's looking for the next team to sponsor?"

"Yeah. And I didn't say anything except to tell him I shop in the kids section."

"I think he senses a winning team." Uncle Leonard claps me on the shoulder as I stand. The softness in his eyes looks so familiar, I get an ache in my throat.

"Yeah. Now we really need to up our training. Wouldn't that be something to win the White Wolf?" I take off the dogs' harnesses as I look over at Cook's team. A new plan starts to form.

3

SUNDAY

I'M NOT TAKING YOU TO ANOTHER dog yard."
My mom thumps her briefcase down on the kitchen
counter and grabs her cheese and cucumber sandwich
from the fridge. "Jeremy Cook's dogs aren't any better
than the ones you already have. A dog's a dog, Vicky.
And we've already got too many."

"Well, that shows how much you know about

it, since a dog is definitely not a dog." I raise my chin and stare at her.

Every time we have this fight about the dogs, I brace myself. For months now I've been waiting for her to say she wants to move back to Seattle. I can see it in her eyes when she talks about growing up in the city. Whenever Nana calls, I know she's trying to talk Mom into moving closer to her.

She looks at me as if I've just proved her point. "You have sixteen dogs to choose from. I'm sure your uncle can figure out which ones to run in the wolf race."

"The White Wolf. And he doesn't choose, I do. *Dad* taught me to choose." I know it's a dirty card to play, but I do what I have to. And if she tells me we're moving, I already know what I'm going to say. She can move if she wants, but I will choose to stay. The dogs and I are staying, end of discussion.

She presses her lips into a thin line and a heavy silence descends around us. If she knew dogs, she'd see why I need a couple of Cook's leaders. Even just two of his best race leaders may mean all the difference for us. I wish she knew dogs. A cold ache spreads through my body and I miss Dad as if the loss were fresh.

"I don't have time for this today." Mom breaks the stalemate with a slump of her shoulders. "I have to work."

"Of course you do."

"Make sure you do your homework," she says, ignoring my tone. "And can you make dinner for us? I should be home around five."

Mom grabs her gear for the open house, sees my sixth-place ribbon from yesterday on the table, and hesitates. She turns back to me. "Oh, Vicky. I'm sorry I forgot to ask you how your race went. You did well."

I shrug. She looks tired and drawn, her eyes peering out of sunken sockets. I suddenly notice how much older she seems, as if she's aged a lifetime this past year. Well, so have I.

She opens her mouth as if she's going to say

something, then runs a hand through her graying blond hair and turns away. Our conversations have stuttered like this since the coffee shop incident.

The bell hanging from the doorknob tinkles and I'm alone.

The dogs outside begin a howl, the song gaining strength as all the dogs join in. I can pick out the individual voices. Bean isn't hard to pick with that awful bawling—his version of a howl. He's got a little too much hound in him. Drift's voice is gorgeous, full and throaty like a wolf howl.

Listening to them makes me more determined to carry out my plan with or without Mom's support. Her car crunches over the snow as she backs out of the driveway, leaving the dog truck just sitting there. I can't talk Cook down in price over the phone; I need to do it in person. And I need to check out all his dogs. I wish Uncle Leonard wasn't going ice fishing today, but I don't need him either. I can get to Cook's myself. Really, what does a couple more years matter?

It's not as if I don't know how to handle the truck now. A license is just a piece of paper.

Before I can talk myself out of it, I hurry to the closet to find the topographic maps. I'm not exactly sure which roads to take to get to Cook's. I mentally kick myself again for leaving the race yesterday before I spoke to him. He and Dad were friends, but I've never been to his house.

The dogs' song ends abruptly just as I find the topo map. I lay it out on the kitchen table and bend over, tracing a path with my finger all the way to town — if you could call tiny Spruce River a town — then on to the other side.

I grunt a little in annoyance. There's really no way I can drive there without traveling the main roads. Any cop who happens to glance over and see what looks like a nine-year-old peering over the steering wheel will surely pull me over.

I finger the chicken-pock scar beside my ear. Maybe I don't need the truck. If I follow the trail network behind the dog yard until the power line, I could cut through the brush there, hook on to the trappers' trails, and eventually get to Cook's. If I drive, the trip is maybe fifty miles, but cross-country it's more like thirty-five. One good thing about living in the Tanana Valley, there's lots of trails to run.

I glance out the window at Bean. He's standing on top of his house, watching me. Reading my mind. Our eyes connect and he throws his head back and barks a command to go. We really need to get to Cook's today. He has champion dogs. If I wait too long, someone else will get there and I'll lose my chance at the best picks. Having a champion team will be a good reason to stay in Alaska. Hard for Mom to argue with that. How can I race dogs in the city?

I imagine crossing the finish line of the White Wolf in first place. *Secord Kennels— that's Michael Secord's daughter, isn't it?* they'd say. *He was a real musher; he taught her well.*

Mom has never understood.

It will take less than four hours of running if the trails are hard—longer with the cut through the brush. We'd keep it easy after the long run yesterday, but we could go and be back before it gets dark. I'd tell Mom we'd been gone for a regular training run. Yeah, one where we found a few extra dogs.

I grab the map and sprint up the stairs to my room. I have to push on the door to move aside the books and gear on the floor. My closet doors haven't been able to shut for years due to my gear collection: tent, Therm-a-Rest, insulated pants, sleeping bags, camp stove. I glance over the pile assessing what I'll need. Extra woollies, dry socks. Should I bring a sleeping bag? It's not that far.

When I was younger, I went on what was supposed to be a short run with Dad. We didn't make it back home until the middle of the night and as I sat shivering but silent in the sled, he muttered over and over, "Why didn't I bring the sleeping bag?"

I take the bag.

I throw everything in a duffel and stop in the kitchen just long enough to grab some snacks.

Go hungry—get cold. I can almost hear Dad's words over my shoulder.

The bag is heavy as I lug it to the yard.

When I step outside, the dogs erupt into a frenzy of high-pitched screams and barks. I feel like a rock star with sixteen adoring fans.

Bean studies me while I pack the sled bag. It's a dark blue, thick canvas bag that's fitted to the dimensions of the sled. The plastic sled bottom makes up the floor, and the sides reach up to attach to lines going from the handlebar down to the brush bow. The top flap is sealed shut with Velcro and keeps most of the snow and ice off the gear inside. I give Mr. Minky a squeeze hello.

"Hey, Bean, want to go on an adventure?"

He stares at me with expressive, ice-blue eyes. His tail wags slowly.

Straddling the dog, I slip a harness over his head

and he punches his legs through the openings. His coarse reddish-brown fur quivers in the places it sticks up over his shoulders and ruff. We lurch over to the sled and I hook him in lead. He leans into his tugline, holding the gangline tight behind him, and barks down the trail.

I hook up Blue, Whistler, Dorset, Drift, and Gazoo, each dog adding a decibel to the frantic barking. Hookups are always wild. The dogs are so jazzed to run; their mouths foam, their eyes sparkle, the air vibrates with an intensity that raises the hairs on my neck.

I yank the snub rope that's tied to the spruce beside me and pull the snow hook. The sled takes off as if I've just punched the hyperdrive button. Each dog in the team instantly stops barking and starts pulling, focused on the trail ahead. The noise behind me from the dogs I didn't take fades fast as we whip through the trees.

4

I GRIP THE HANDLEBAR AS I LEAN into a turn. We skid sideways with a fan of snow. The dogs' feet kick up tufts of ice crystals as they dig, and the cold wind on my face energizes me. I let out a whoop, feeling savage. Watching them run gives me such a visceral sense of belonging, I can't imagine being anywhere else. Bean swivels his ears back toward me but keeps running straight down the trail.

"It's all right, Beanie. Keep ahead, that a boy!"

I wish I could talk Sarah into coming along. It would let me spend more time with her, and I'd get to show her how amazing my dogs are. Why wouldn't everyone in my class want to see this? Uncle Leonard says dogsledding is a dying art. That it's too much work for most kids and I'll soon see it isn't the popular kids from school that end up worth anything, but the ones who are brave enough to be different. He has to say that, being Dad's twin brother.

We follow our own trail until we arrive at the fork where it veers into the main snowmobile track. The trail is lined with shrubby willows and spruce. Crystallized snow piled on the branches contrasts with the sea of pale and dark greens.

The Cooks, Mr. Oleson, and I all use this trail sometimes to run our teams together so we can practice passing and leading. Mr. Oleson is our closest neighbor; he lives a subsistence lifestyle in the bush with his dogs, his garden, and his gun. He doesn't race, but he likes to run with other mushers. Sometimes he used our yurt. Most mushers around here use these portable, round tents for base camps. But our yurt has been taken down. My hands clench the handlebar when I think of Mom selling it to Cook.

"Vicky, you can't set up a yurt yourself. And I don't know how to set it up. It may as well be used by someone who needs it."

I couldn't argue with that, but it still felt like selling off a piece of Dad.

Running with Cook's dogs is how I know they're stars. I press my lips together as I think of all the years Dad raced, and not once did he come in first. He said he probably never would with trapline dogs. Why didn't he get a couple sleek racers then? Well, now I have that opportunity, so I have to do it for him. The need to do something for him burns behind my eyes.

After an hour of solid running, we arrive at another fork.

"Gee, Bean . . . that's it, Blue! Good boys!" We veer right. Good command leaders like Bean know their right—gee, from their left—haw. The dogs charge down the trail. We don't usually run this way and they love exploring.

I glance up and notice the darkening sky. There's a hazy ring around the sun—a sun dog. If I look for it, I can see the little prisms of color. There's snow on the way and I forgot to check the forecast before I left. Crap.

Hopefully we'll be back home by the time it gets too thick. But first, we should take a break. To slow the team down, I step on the strip of snowmobile track that's hanging between the runners. It bites into the snow.

"Whoa, whoa . . . good dogs." I throw the snow hook down and stomp on it.

Gazoo dives into the deep snow on the side of

the trail and chomps mouthfuls of fluff. I dab at the base of my cold nose with the back of my glove. After many chapped lips, I've learned to stop licking away the salty runoff. I walk up the line, patting each dog.

Bean rolls on the trail scratching his back, all four feet waving in the air. In the quiet of being far away from anywhere, the only sounds are the grunts and soft snufflings of the dogs. I take a moment to close my eyes and listen to the world around me.

Savor it.

The trees are still with hardly a breeze. We're beside a stand of tamaracks, my favorite trees. Their needles, soft green in summer, burst with vivid yellows in fall, and then drop off leaving them to stand naked in winter. An evergreen that isn't always green. A tree that's different.

A gray jay's sharp trill makes me jump and open my eyes. I pull out the map from the pocket of my anorak. Our route will take us along this trail several more miles before we cut across to the trapper's trail.

"You up for a little cross-country, Blue?"

He looks up at me with his mismatched eyes. One soft brown, the other frenetic blue. I like to imagine this makes him able to see the world in two ways. Maybe see both sides of an argument. He certainly seems to switch easily from goofy to serious. His wide-mouthed grin is fringed in an icy rime.

"Deep snow will make extra work," I say.

He pokes his nose between my legs and pushes until his head is wedged under my butt. I laugh at his favorite game and scratch his back. He leans into my hands until he nearly topples over.

When I head back to the sled, the dogs stand and watch me behind them. I climb onto the runners and bend to the hook.

"Ready?" My foot presses on the snowmobile track as I hang the snow hook in front of me. The dogs scream and jump in the air. "All right!"

They leap forward in unison and we take off again running flat out down the trail. Then they settle into a ground-eating trot. I reach into the sled bag and pull out the insulated water bottle, take a sip, and put it back. It's so easy to get dehydrated out here.

The willow thickets lining the trail along this stretch all look the same. It's hard to tell where we should try to cut across to the other trail. So finally, I just call haw and we veer left and stop at the tree line. My stomach flutters a little with the excitement at doing something new. I have to make sure that I don't make any mistakes out here. I pull out my round bear-paw snowshoes, the kind without tails so it's easier to back up or turn around, and then take a bearing with my compass.

"Okay, guys, you can follow me now."

The snowshoes punch through deep drifts as I head into the trees. I glance over my shoulder and see the dogs jumping behind me like marten through the snow. The lower tree branches droop beneath the weight of their loads. Everywhere I look is white powdery freshness.

Each movement is deliberate with my large shoes. My feet sink down a little as I step, and I flick my ankles to knock the snow from the webbing. Bean continuously jumps on the backs of them.

"Get back, you little turds." I rub Bean's head affectionately.

After about half an hour I stop and peel off my hat to keep from over heating. The sun has disappeared now behind a dull gray and the air is suddenly choked with snow. I thought I had much more time before it started. A tendril of worry snakes into my gut.

I take out the map again while the dogs mill around me, and brush off the fat flakes that immediately cover it.

"We should be there by now," I say, trying not to sound concerned. The last thing a sled dog wants to hear is hesitation from his leader.

While I'm studying the map I notice I'm holding my breath, and let it out in a rush. The frozen cloud hangs in front of my face. I glance up with eyes half closed to shield them from the snow floating down and melting on my face.

Where is the trail? I check my compass again and take a bearing on the tallest spruce ahead.

When I take another step forward, I pitch into the snow. "Oof! Bean! Get off my snowshoe!"

Bean and Blue jump me while I'm down and the snowshoes flail in the air as I roll around pushing at furry dog legs. I feel as if I'm trying to surface in a pool of quicksand as I sink in the soft, deep snow. An icy trail of snow trickles down my neck. Bean offers to help by cleaning out my ear.

When I finally roll to my feet, I keep my voice light for them. "Let's go find that trail."

We plod onward. Finally, I see a break in the trees ahead. *The trail!*

I whoop and punch my fist in the air. Just as we're about to reach it, a lime green object shines in the trees. What is that?

Creeping closer, I finally recognize what it is—a

snowmobile. And it's pretty thoroughly wrapped itself around a birch. There's no one around and no footprints in the snow. I stomp onto the trail and take off my snowshoes. Once I string the dogs out straight, I set the snow hook.

Where the heck did the snowmobile come from? Who drove it here and left it? How did they leave without footprints? I wander behind the sled and scan the woods.

"Hello?" I call. Then louder, "Anyone here?"

The dogs watch me with intent eyes, heads tilting. The falling snow mutes any sounds and closes in on me as if I'm in a padded room. It feels as if it's just me and the dogs in all the world. Except for whoever was on that snowmobile. My traitorous mind suddenly envisions a psycho creeping up behind me in the silence, and I spin around with my heart pounding.

"Stupid! Get a grip." I scan the ground, but the fat flakes are laying a cover over everything so perhaps the footprints have been hidden.

Blue lets out a bark, and that's when I whip around and finally see him.

Crumpled in a heap several yards from the sled is a man lying face down. I stumble past a black helmet that's been smashed in the visor. It's not until I kneel beside him that I see all the blood.

"Oh! Not good, not good, not good."

Now that I'm closer, I see he's not a man, but a boy about my age. I stare at all the blood starkly red against the snow, and my mind freezes for a moment. I wish Dad were here to tell me what to do. But I'm the only one around.

Bean croons at me long and low. When my focus snaps toward him, my head clears, kicking into gear. I set my mouth in a determined line and take a deep breath.

5

BLOOD COVERS MOST OF HIS FACE but I can still tell I've never seen him before. I move to turn him over, then stop, thinking about first-aid classes and not moving someone with a suspected head injury. I bend closer and feel for a pulse along his neck. A soft breath warms my cheek and I let out my own with relief.

I lurch back to the sled and brush off the layer of

snow that has built up on the bag. Tearing open the Velcro, I dive into the gear, searching for the first-aid kit.

What to do? *Think, think, think.*

Snow continues to build in the air and falls in thick sheets, turning my whole world white. In fact, I can hardly see the snowmobile's tracks. Which way did he come? Should I leave him here and go get help? No, he'll freeze. But I can't move him to put him in the sled bag.

I kneel down beside him again and use a handful of snow to wipe the blood from his face. More blood seeps from a gash above his right eyebrow, contrasting with the chalky white of his face. I'd probably freak out with all the blood if I hadn't helped Dad on his trapline since I could walk.

I wipe the new blood away to inspect the gash. He's wearing a ski jacket and blue jeans. Jeans? Obviously he doesn't get out much. They're thoroughly soaked, and now will only make things worse for him. He's going to freeze for sure.

I run through a mental list as I find a large gauze pad in the kit. First, I need to stop the bleeding.

Scooting closer to his head, I take a quick breath and press the gauze to his gash. He moans and rolls his head away. His eyes open and we stare at each other.

"What . . . what happened?" His voice is small and thin.

"You crashed your snowmobile into a tree."

He struggles to a sitting position, and looks around. He raises his hand to his head and pulls it away, looking at the blood on his glove.

"Yeah, I was just getting to that. You're still bleeding."

"I have to get home!" He tries to stand but his face goes even whiter and he crumples back onto the snow.

I reach for him. "Take it easy. Slow down." Where is his home? I wonder. Who is he?

"Where did you come from?"

"Um . . . " He jerks his head around, grabs at it as

if it made him dizzy, and closes his eyes. "That way." He points down the trail behind him.

"You came from that direction? You're sure not from there?" I point in the opposite direction.

He opens his eyes again and they seem more focused. He looks into my face and shakes his head a tiny bit. "No." He fingers his forehead gingerly.

"How far is it to your house?"

"Not far. I think."

I rock back on my heels. Should I bring him back on the trail that I came from? It's pretty far, plus there's the hike through the trees. I dab at the base of my nose. He'd have to get out of the sled and walk through the deep snow. What he needs is to get warm and dry in a hurry. But I'm not sure if we should go the way he says he came from. I haven't been on that trail before. What if we get lost?

I don't know what to do.

Through the swirling flakes, I peer north at the trail he pointed to. Then I look back the other way.

I could maybe take the south trail like I'd planned and see if we can make it to Cook's. I'm guessing it's another ten miles though. And there's this blizzard building. I let out a long breath. Sounds as if his place is closer.

"Okay, we better get going before it's dark . . . but your head." I hold up the gauze. "We have to stop the bleeding."

He takes the gauze and presses it to his head, wincing as he looks at me. "Feels great," he says with a half-smile.

My shoulders slump forward to see him smile. He must not be hurt as bad as it looks if he's smiling. Head wounds always bleed a lot, I remember from first-aid class. As I tape the gauze into place a suspicious thought suddenly hits me. Why is he smiling when he has a head wound? I narrow my eyes a bit to study him again. His face is square and open with the hint of stubble on his upper lip. A dimple in his left cheek deepens with his grin.

"If you live close, how come I've never met you? What's your name?"

"My name?" He blinks at me with confusion and he looks so vulnerable that I immediately feel dumb for asking. "It's Chris."

It's not as if I know every single person in town. Lots of kids bus to Fairbanks for school. Larger centers offer more programs than my tiny rural school, Spruce River High. I shake my head and resolve to stop watching slasher movies.

I unwrap the scarf from around my neck and tie it around his head to cover the gauze. His dark brown hair flops over the top across his forehead.

"How do I look?"

The scarf is red and covered with black dog paw prints. He looks a little like a pirate, but I ignore his question. I help him stand and have to crane my head to see him towering over me. My head comes to his armpits.

He sways back on his feet, leans on me, and staggers to the sled. Then he seems to notice the dogs for the first time.

"Augh! Where's your sled?"

"This is my sled."

"No, your real sled. Your snowmobile." His voice cracks slightly.

"This is way better than a snowmobile," I say. "It doesn't wrap itself around trees." But then I remember the time I did break the brush bow on a tree that had jumped in front of us and Dad lectured me for days about being too reckless. I argued right back that the dogs were completely fine, so what was the big deal? If I could take back every argument I had with Dad, I would.

The dogs bark with excitement when they see us moving toward the sled. Chris shrinks back and glances around with cornered eyes.

"Um, I don't think they like me." His gaze darts from me to the dogs, then back to my face. He seems to study me, as if recognizing me from somewhere.

"They don't even care about you. They're not barking because they want to attack, they just want to run. Huskies aren't guard dogs." My words are harsher than I intended, but I stand tall ready to defend them. Part of me wishes for the easy way that Sarah has of talking to boys. Maybe I need to start spending more time with other people like she keeps telling me.

"Anyway, just get in. We've got to hurry." I push him down into the sled bag and run back for my first-aid kit. The dogs scream and lunge forward, and I jump on the runners just as the snow hook pops.

The dogs immediately fall silent as we lurch ahead. I lean forward to make sure Chris is settled. He's perched on top of the gear, sitting upright with his knees bent and his head and shoulders leaning back against the handlebar. One hand grips the side of the sled bag, and the other awkwardly presses on his bandage. He stares at me with wide eyes. I gesture with the top flap of the bag to get him to tuck it around himself to keep the snow out.

We head into a narrow, twisty section of trail and I have to concentrate. The extra weight in the sled slows us so it's harder to steer around trees. Snow falls steadily, so thick that it shrouds Bean and Blue from my view. I glance behind us and notice our tracks are covered almost as soon as we make them.

This trail is out of Dad's old trapping area. I've never been here, preferring to stick to the trails I know. I'm relying on Chris to lead so when we get to a fork I ask which way and Chris says left and that's what we do. At another fork we go right and after nearly an hour of narrow corners and fallen trees, my apprehensions about Chris returns. How could he have come through here with his snowmobile? And why?

6

JUST AS I NOTICE THAT I'M squinting to see through the gloom ahead, we break out of the trees into a marshy area dotted with black spruce. Snow fills the air like a swarm of bees stinging exposed skin. Now that we're in the open, I realize how much the wind has picked up. I hunch my shoulders to cover my bare neck.

"Are you sure we're going the right way?" I glance down and notice with alarm that Chris's eyes are closed and his face is pasty. "Hey, are you all right?"

"B–b–brilliant." His blue lips quiver as he talks.

What am I doing? He's hit his head and he's just going to get worse if I don't start thinking. He needs to lie still, not jerk around in a dogsled. And he has to get warm. Right now. I stop the team and set the hook.

"Good dogs." I grab the picket line from beside Chris in the sled bag. "Stay in the bag for a minute. I have to settle the team."

I string the cable between two spruce trees, and then unhook the dogs one at a time to transfer them to the drop lines on the cable picket. Each dog scratches and sniffs and circles around in the deep snow as if this is a perfectly fine place to catch a nap. Whistler waves her butt in front of Gazoo and then snaps at him when he pokes his nose too close. My heart swells with what a good job they've done today and how hard they've worked. They're going to need snacks.

I turn back to the sled, and bend to help Chris out. "We'll stay here a while — maybe it'll stop snowing."

He wobbles and leans heavily on me. He smells like winter.

When he's got his footing, I sort through my gear. "I'm going to make a fire . . . there's a sleeping bag in here somewhere . . . you'll be warm then . . . where is it? Ah, you were sitting on it."

I pull out the bag and send a silent thank you to Dad for reminding me to bring it. Once I've grabbed the rest of the gear we need, I close the sled bag so snow doesn't get in.

"You g-g-got a hot tub in there?" He stands with his arms wrapped around himself.

I know you start getting confused with the onset of hypothermia. He doesn't realize how serious this is.

"Or maybe a cell phone?"

"Cell phones don't work out here." I hack spruce boughs off the trees with my hatchet and spread them out, making a thick pile under the hanging branches of another spruce. "Perhaps if you were dressed properly . . . " I hear the condescending tone in my voice and try again. "You'll have to take off those stupid jeans, they're wet and only making you colder." I hold up my spare woollies. "I'm not sure these will fit, but they stretch."

"Th-they're pink."

"Yeah, present from my mom. Sorry 'bout that, but beggars can't be choosers." The sleeping bag crunches in the cold as I pull it out of the stuff sack. "Come sit here."

He slumps down on the branches and takes the bag with shaking hands. When he tries to climb in, I see how uncoordinated he is. I squat down and help him into the bag, flipping the hood over his head and zipping it up to his chin.

"We've just met and you're already t-trying to get me in the s-sack."

I stare at him. He either thinks he's charming, or when he hit his head, he damaged his social skills.

I open my mouth, then think better of it and push the water bottle at him. "I'm going to collect firewood. Stay here. Drink. And take off those jeans."

He burrows into his cocoon and I slide the sled beside him as a windbreak. With the trees at his back cutting the south wind, and the sled bag blocking the swirling winds from the west, it should be a warm enough spot once I get a fire going.

Southwest winds. I curse myself for not paying attention to this. They usually bring storms.

As I break off dead branches, I remember winter camping with Dad. "That's it, Vic," he had said. "These spruce needles will be good for insulation under our tent. And the bark off the birch makes a natural fire starter. We have everything we need to survive right here."

One ice-fishing trip we camped just for fun. We

stayed for three nights. When we took down the tent, the melted indents in the snow where our bodies had slept proved he was right; the spruce needles underneath had kept us warm. But in the end, all the bush knowledge in the world couldn't help Dad.

Because I wasn't there.

I close my eyes and tap my forehead with the back of my glove, and then light the pile of tinder I'd gathered. I hang over the flame, using my body as a windbreak, and coax it to grow by feeding it some bigger sticks. It's amazing how much better everything seems with a fire. It pops and sparks and immediately warms the skin on my neck and face.

Whistler lets loose a long, slow howl. Seconds later, the other five point their muzzles in the air —black lips ringing in an O. The song undulates and wavers with layers of different voices. As if the conductor had waved his arms in finale, all the dogs stop at the same time. I always wonder how they do that.

"Whoa." Chris is staring at the dogs from his sleeping bag. I notice his lips look better—less blue.

"They're hungry after all that work saving you."

"Well tell them I'm not that tasty. Pretty stringy actually. Why is the big ugly one staring at me?"

Ugly? "Listen, genius, my dogs are the only things that are important right now. They're going to haul both of us out of here, so they deserve some respect." He obviously doesn't know a good dog when he sees one.

"Whoa," he says again, arching his brows. "Sorry, they seem like very nice dogs with big teeth. You haven't even told me your name."

I grab the bag with the fist-size chicken chunks and march over to the dogs. "Victoria Secord," I yell over the dogs' demanding screams.

"Longoria?"

"Victoria." I toss a chunk to Dorset. She snaps it from the air and turns her back on Blue, who's reaching for me with front paws outstretched.

"Victoria Secret?"

Oh, so annoying. "You're hilarious." I sweep my arm toward the dogs. "I race sled dogs. I'm one of the top junior mushers." I'm not sure why I feel the need to tell him this.

"Oh, yeah! I thought I recognized you. I saw you yesterday at the race." He takes a swig from the water bottle and wipes his mouth with the back of his glove. "The pink tights fit, but they're a little short. They only go to my knees."

I bite my lip to keep from laughing and turn away. "You were at the race?"

I throw a chunk to Blue, who has worked himself up to such a frenzy that he has to put the chunk between his feet and pant over it before he can start to gnaw.

"Yeah, Mom and I went to check it out. Some

jerk sideswiped us, though. Took the mirror off my mom's Chevette."

I blink. "Uh, sideswiped? You see who did it?"

"No, happened when we were parked—"

Chris is interrupted by Drift, who screams as if someone is ripping off her toenails. I toss her a chunk and she grabs it expertly from the air.

"So . . . " I change the subject. "Which school do you go to? Fairbanks?"

"I'll be starting at Spruce River High on Monday. I'm a sophomore . . . er . . . that was the plan. So I'm guessing I'll have the privilege of your cheery personality greeting me in the halls?"

He grins and I almost smile at how ridiculous he looks, sitting up with his broad shoulders stuffed into the bag and the red scarf tied lopsided around his head. Flickering light from the fire glows on his face. When he turns to me, I notice the startling colors in his deep-set hazel eyes.

A gust of wind blows sparks and snow pellets

against both of us. Chris tilts his head and shuts his eyes. He tucks farther into the bag.

"So, why did you start racing sled dogs? I mean, it's cool, but sort of different."

"I like being different." My voice sounds a little too loud. "And it's not that different. Lots of kids my age race."

I try and think of something profound to say about why I run dogs. About how I'd been around dogs my whole life with Dad and how I can understand them. How I feel alive when I run them, how they take me to a magical place that I can get to only behind a team. And how running the dogs makes me feel close to Dad.

"And I like racing." Less profound than I wanted. "I'm good at it."

I give up and add more wood to the fire.

Chris shrugs and huddles closer to the flames. Falling snow swirls around him and I suddenly notice how dark it is. And cold.

7

I GIVE THE REST OF THE DOGS their meal and pick up the hatchet again. Judging by the cloaking darkness settling in, I'd say it's around six thirty. During the winter months, the only thing I hate is the short days. Now that we're into March, the stretching daylight feels like a gift.

With the approaching gloom and the blowing

snow, I can hardly see beyond the pale light the fire is giving. The trees around us appear as one black blob. The wind gusts noisily through the branches. When I look up, I see the tops of the spruce whipping around like angry fists shaking at the sky.

I hack off more boughs from the closest spruce and carry them over to the dogs, who rest just on the edge of the fire light. They jump up when I approach. I lay the boughs in a flat pile next to the dogs, making sure the layers overlap to give them insulation. Dorset sticks her tongue up my nose when I bend over her. Blue grabs the branches to arrange his own way, then spins in two circles and flops down on top of them, tail curling over his black snout.

I whisper to Bean, "We're going to have to stay here."

The tension of this thought travels up my spine and tightens my neck muscles. I rock from one foot to the other. I'll have to find enough firewood for the evening and water the dogs somehow. And feed us. I stretch my neck from side to side.

It's okay, I try to tell myself. It's not as if I've never slept out in the woods before. Plus, I've spent enough time alone on the race trail with just my dogs. In fact, that's how I prefer it. My dogs always understand me.

And it's not as if there's a horde of people lined up to come along.

Uncle Leonard says I'm a loner because I'm an only child. I would have had brothers and sisters but, as Dad says, I came out fighting and something happened when I was born that made Mom unable to have any more kids.

Mom doesn't have brothers or sisters either and she likes to do weird things by herself, like go to the movies. She's been doing that even more this past year, just leaving by herself. Well, she used to ask me to come, but after the coffee shop incident, she stopped.

I close my eyes and rub between them, as if I can rub away the memory.

"What do you want, Vicky?" she'd asked me.

"I don't care." We were sitting in the booth farthest away from the only other people in the shop. I was staring at the sign on the wall: COFFEE. DO STUPID STUFF FASTER AND WITH MORE ENERGY.

"Well, you must have an opinion? How about a hot chocolate?" Her voice had sounded strained. Brightly fake. She leaned across the table and smiled at me. A blue vein under her eye twitched.

"Sure."

We didn't say anything else until our orders were ready. Then we probably should've kept on saying nothing. But we didn't.

Mom: Oh, I can't tell you how much I love this chai tea. Something about the smell of it reminds me of when I used to go out with your Nana and we'd shop and have mother-daughter time.

Me: Huh.

Her: So. Tell me how school's going.

Me: Fine.

Her: How is Mr. Mowat's new baby?

Me: Great.

Her: Sarah's mom told me his wife brought her in to the school for a visit.

Me: I don't know.

And that's when she did it. That's when Mom reached across to take my hand and I jumped back, knocking my hot chocolate over. It was as if the brown liquid pouring out of the cup and running onto the floor was rushing to escape.

"Look." I started in what may have been a whisper. I think. But it didn't stay as a whisper. "I don't know why we're pretending everything is okay. It's *not* okay and it never will be okay. Ever. So don't act like we're carrying on with our lives. I don't want to sit around pretending to be your buddy! You never understood the dogs. You never understood *him!*" I shrieked the last part, but managed to cut myself off from saying what was next. *And whose fault is it that he's gone?* But the damage was already done. The color drained from my mom's face. Her eyes went red, welled up, looked away.

I don't think she's really looked at me since.

I pick up some branches, but then drop them again. I could use that cup of hot chocolate now, that's for sure. And I wouldn't mind having Sarah here. To talk to. She's good at talking about things.

Bean sniffs deeply into his branches, then snorts with feeling. I smile at my leader. He's even better than Sarah — not that I would tell her that. He just listens. Makes me feel calm. Since the accident, I'm happier when I'm with the dogs. They don't pity or judge.

But usually when I'm out on the trail, I don't have to worry about having enough food. I trudge back to the sled, and then pull it closer under the spruce. Chris glances at me as I sit on the brush bow. The fire spits and embers fly into the air when I poke it with a stick. I lift my chin. The heat coming off the fire helps my mind focus on what I need to do.

"Here." I offer my sandwich to Chris and his eyes light up. He tears the saran off and takes a huge bite.

"Mmm, so good." He practically inhales the rest. "That was awesome. Thanks. What else you got?"

"Maybe we can find you some yellow birch twigs to chew," I say, around a mouthful of Fig Newton. "They taste like spearmint. Very healthy."

"We must be close to my place. We can feast when we get there. I can't wait to show you my warm kitchen."

I study him closely. He's still shivering. "Well, it won't be tonight." I drink from my spare water bottle and watch the dogs curled on their little nests in the snow. Bean has one eye open checking to see what I'm doing.

"You mean we're going—we're going to stay out here? All night?" Chris's voice is edged in panic. "In the winter?"

"You say that like you've never spent the night outside before."

"I'm more of an indoor adventure type."

"Uh-huh. Well, it'll be too dangerous to travel in this blizzard. We'll have to stick it out here."

Chris paws at his jacket, peering in the pockets and glancing around. "I—uh, I must've left my GPS back on my machine. Where's yours?"

"I just have a compass and topo." I stand and pull the map from my pocket. Chris grabs it and leans toward the light of the fire. His brows furrow and his mouth is set in a tight line.

"There's a creek or slough over there," I say, and point my chin to the open area that is completely obscured with falling and blowing snow. Maybe Chris will tell me we're just around the corner from his house. "You look for this slough on the map and I'll go find us some water."

"What's a slough?"

Or maybe not. "It's like a branch off a river." Why doesn't he know that?

I sort through the back pouch of the sled bag

until I find the rope. I tie one end around my wrist and one to the sled. When I pick up the headlamp and slide it over my hat, I'm reminded of Dad telling me that out here, even a light can't tame the wild.

Sometimes, the wild is sleeping and you get lulled into a trance. But it doesn't stay sleeping for long in winter. You have to pay attention all the time and be ready for when it wakes up howling. When I click on the light, I'm in a whirlpool of snowflakes swirling around my head so fast, it makes me dizzy.

It's howling.

I shut off the light, then turn with both dog dishes in one hand and a long stick in the other, and head toward where I think the water is. The blinding snow combined with the solid darkness makes it tough to walk. I stagger on my feet as I poke the uneven ground.

Fear rushes through me but I try to ignore it. The irrational phobia I've had of water my whole life definitely gets in my way. I take deep breaths to get my thoughts under control and focus on feeling the terrain under my mukluks. I can't afford weakness now.

When I hear sloshing under my feet, I stop and dip the dishes into the slushy water. Handy that I don't have to chop through ice. That's one of the perks of this area — surrounded by mountains, dotted with frozen black spruce bogs, criss-crossed with rivers and sloughs. There's usually water available.

When I turn, I search for the glow of the fire. All I see is a wall of white against the blackness surrounding me. I can't even tell which direction to walk in. My legs shake with the knowledge of our situation.

As I get closer following the rope, relief shoots through me when I see the fire and the silhouettes of the dogs.

Of course they're where I left them. I shake my head at being such a pansy.

Chris is hunched over the flame. When he sees me, he shifts his back to me and wiggles slightly. My curiosity over what he's doing is interrupted when the end of the sleeping bag is kicked practically into the fire.

I leap for it. "Don't get too close, you'll burn the bag!" I snatch the end and inspect it.

"Okay, okay." Chris gathers the bag tighter and holds it closed at his neck. "Not that I'm ungrateful for the designer pants, or the five-star accommodations"—he glances at the dogs—"or the presence of the man-eaters over there . . . I mean, it's really cool you're, like, this amazing bushwoman and all, but . . . don't you notice—it's getting rippin' cold out?"

"Since I'm doing all the work, no. I haven't had time to get cold."

He still has the scarf around his head, but his face has color now. The strain of worrying about that finally leaves the pit of my stomach. Now all I have to worry about is freezing to death, feeding us, feeding the dogs, and finding our way home. Oh, and the heart attack Mom is probably having because I'm late.

8

I SET THE METAL DISHES BESIDE THE fire and plop a chunk of chicken in one. Chris looks at it in disgust.

"Oh, that's disturbing. I think I'll go with the birch twigs, please."

"Good thing this isn't for you then." I make sure to hide my smile. "I mentioned before, the dogs worked hard for you and they need to be watered."

I've never been called an amazing bushwoman by anyone other than maybe my uncle. Uncle Leonard keeps telling me that I can't do everything. I need to let people help me. But I am the only one who my dogs can count on now. Uncle Leonard also tells me I should be nicer to Mom.

I stab at the chicken with a stick to try and melt it quicker. The fire crackles, filling the silence between me and Chris. I rise to collect more wood while the chicken thaws.

I'm avoiding thinking about our nighttime sleeping arrangements. When I run a race, I sleep in the sled bag. It makes a great shelter from the snow and wind and is just long and wide enough for me to lie down in. But I really can't say "night" to Chris, climb into the sled bag, and then just close it up, leaving him under the tree. Not unless I want to see a Chris-sicle frozen solid in the morning.

Once the water is warm, I divide the chicken into six and serve a portion to Bean. He drinks eagerly and licks up the last of the bloody gobs from the side of the dish. I take the empty dish and collect more water.

Between collecting firewood and watering the dogs, I manage to avoid the Chris problem until it's so cold, my nose hairs freeze together if I breathe too deeply.

I visit with each dog once more, petting and whispering in their ears. I put the dog jackets — fleece liners with windstopper nylon shells — on Bean and Dorset. They don't have the thick natural coats the rest of the dogs have. A dog like Drift would just eat the jacket anyway if I left her with it overnight.

As soon as I'm done, the dogs curl up and look like giant versions of the coconut rum balls Mom used to make at Christmas. They seem content with the firelight catching their eyes and making them shine. In truth, I need them a lot more than they need me. The shame of this heats my face.

Chris is leaning toward the fire again and I smell the singed bag. "It's too cold out here."

I sort of admire how he's not afraid to show what a complete tadpole he is.

The wind is screaming through the clearing, pelting snow and cold into me, looking for chinks in my armor. I raise my shoulders to try and protect the heat escaping out my exposed neck. Black, cold, winter night. Deadly night.

"Shouldn't we build an igloo or something?" Chris brushes off the snow that continually coats the sleeping bag.

Once I trudge to the sled, I hold Mr. Minky in my left hand, feel its familiar, comforting shape under my gloved fingers, and clear my throat. "We're going to hole up in the sled until morning." I look at the bag when I speak, but sense his stare. His fear seems to have vanished suddenly.

"Ah-ha, I knew you were trying—"

"We'll be warmer in there out of the snow and wind. It's like a small tent." I open the sled bag and look inside. *So small.*

More doubts and unhelpful movie titles like *Swamp Thing,* and *Sleeping with the Enemy* swarm in my head. I notice I'm holding my arms across myself, and drop them, standing up straighter.

I seriously need to get out more. I swear I'll start going to those lame house parties that Sarah keeps insisting I go to. "For your rep," she says. "You're in danger of becoming one of those crazy old dog ladies who never partied when she was young and wrinkle-free, and then lives to regret it for the rest of her life."

I love her like she's a sister, but only Sarah could worry about getting wrinkles.

Chris stands, wobbles a little, then leans over the sled to look in. He holds the sleeping bag up to his chest as if he's ready to enter a potato-sack race. Our eyes meet across the sled bag. He smiles.

"After you," he says.

"We have to lay our outer clothes down on the bottom; they'll dry with our body heat."

74

Chris opens his mouth to say something, but then just grins wider.

I ignore him and slide the sled onto the spruce boughs. My throat catches when I try to swallow. I take off my anorak.

"You should, um, get in first. You're bigger." My hands tremble and I'm glad it's too dark for him to notice.

"It's about the size of a coffin in here, isn't it?" Chris climbs in and lies down with his knees bent awkwardly. His shoulders take up the width of the sled.

"Put your jacket under the sleeping bag," I say loudly over the wind, as I shuck off my snow pants. My stomach flips.

"Move over." I try to sound nonchalant, as if I do this all the time, sleep in my sled with some dude I've just met. I take off my wool pants, and throw them into the bottom of the sled.

Chris unzips the sleeping bag and holds it open

for me. His teeth flash white in the dark like a Cheshire cat. Shivering in my skivvies, I climb in.

"Ow! That's my hip!"

"Well, move your hip."

"Augh, your elbow is digging into my ribs . . ."

"Don't . . . would you stop that . . . ouch . . . your knee . . ."

We squirm around until we find that the best place for me is under his arm, spooning with my back to him. I zip the sleeping bag to block out the cold, and reach up to close the sled bag over us, leaving a breathing hole for the condensation to escape.

The relief from the cold is immediate. It feels as if I'm lying next to a furnace with the heat that Chris's body is emitting. I don't know why he was complaining when he's so hot.

I almost let out a nervous giggle but manage to get a grip in time.

The wind outside seems to howl in frustration, wanting to get in. The canvas bag flaps while the whole sled quivers. I've always felt as if my sled bag was my secret hideout. Only me in here listening to my dogs sleeping out there. The shape of it, the feel of the rough sides, the smell of wet canvas, it's all comforting and familiar. And now Chris, who I don't even know, is sharing this place with me.

I close my eyes and try to fall asleep. Or imagine that I can actually fall asleep while I'm in the same sleeping bag pressed up next to a guy. His breath feels warm on the back of my neck and I wish that I couldn't smell him. I try to picture what he looks like in my pink woollies, and that helps.

"If you're, like, some axe murderer or something, tell me now so I can sleep with my eyes open," Chris says in the dark.

My eyes fly open. "When we get to school, there will be no one who knows about this."

He muffles a laugh. "Deal."

9

MONDAY

I WAKE TO SPIDER WEBS OF FROST hanging over my face. Unlike some mornings when I'm confused for a moment about where I am, I have an exact understanding of my situation. I'm in a sleeping bag.

With a guy.

I stretch out a sudden leg cramp and Chris jerks awake beside me.

"Don't bang the sides of the bag," I say. "The frost will fall on us."

I carefully reach up and open the sled bag, flipping over the flap of canvas coated with frozen condensation. It's heavy with the snow load on top. Cold air rushes in and I quickly pull my arm back under the sleeping bag.

I could almost fall back to sleep in the warmth. I let my mind drift and enjoy the novelty of the situation.

"Morning, Secret." Chris straightens his arms out in front of him and yawns loudly. "I could sure use some scrambled eggs and bacon."

I roll away from him. "You could use a shower, too. You smell like a sasquatch." This is a big lie.

I resign myself to the freezing air and wriggle out of the bag. The side of my body that was pressed to Chris is now cold. When I stand on the snow-covered spruce branches, I exhale rapidly and clouds of frozen breath hang in the air. My bare fingers move slowly in the chill as I scramble to put on my outer clothes. I hop around to warm up.

"Little brisk out today," I say.

The first thing I check is the dogs. They're still curled into six snowballs, the branches above them covered in glistening frost.

Then I glance around and blink.

The landscape looks completely different from last night. Fresh and friendly with glittering beauty. Now that I can see the slough in the daylight, it doesn't seem that far away. And the blackened ring of the long-dead fire has melted a deep pit in the snow. New snow sparkles all around us. Blankets of clean white snow heap over alder bushes and dark stumps, softening all the edges. I feel as if I've just stepped into a Christmas card. I marvel at how a sunny winter morning always fills me up.

Trees snap and crack in the cold. The wind has died and the hushed winter bush sounds are all around me. I spy the line of snow-covered birches gleaming in the sun and I let out a little breath. Every tiny finger of branch has a thick coating of snow that sits like whipped topping.

"Wake me when it's summer," Chris says.

The snow crunches under my feet as I move. I find a wide tree, check to make sure I can't be seen from the sled, and crouch down to pee. Crunching snow is good. That means the temperature isn't much colder than zero. If the snow squeaks we're in bigger trouble. I'd hate to think about our night if it were January instead.

I check the color of the hole I've made in the snow and smile a little in relief. Light yellow means I've been drinking enough. Only once did I see it a dark amber color. That was during the Fur Classic, just after the accident.

I had fought hard to enter that race, too. And I was desperate to win—to have Dad's name in the papers and on the radio. But I was so sick and useless to the dogs, I had to scratch the whole race. I had thought that by putting all my attention to the dogs' needs, we would win for sure. Checking their feet, pulling down their lower eyelids to see their skin color, snacking them—none of that was enough. Without drinking or eating anything myself, it wasn't long before I hardly had energy to pedal the sled. When I started throwing up, I knew our race was over. I swore that wouldn't happen again.

The snow feels plenty cold as I rub a handful into my bare hands to wash. I quickly scrub my face and then stand, pushing the water off my freezing cheeks. I shake my hands and tuck them in my armpits. My face tingles and the skin pulls when I smile.

"Come on, Chris. We should look at your head."

"Everyone keeps telling me I need my head examined."

I rummage in the bag that hangs from the back of the handlebar. Where did I leave that first-aid kit? "Sounds like you're well enough today to help with the chores. We need another fire to boil water for us and melt some chicken to water the dogs."

"I've got to water a tree first."

I try to remember the last time I saw the kit. Oh yeah, I had it in my anorak pocket with the map — *the map!*

"And seriously, is there like, room service? I'm so hungry, I could eat a dog."

I had completely forgotten about the map last night. Chris was going to show me where he lived. But I never saw it after that. I feel a bubble of panic.

"Chris, what did you do with the map I gave you?"

"What map?"

"The *map*. The map I gave you last night, remember?" The panic bubble expands.

"Um . . . I don't remember you giving me a map." Chris's head pops up from the sled bag and he glances around as if he's looking for it.

"You said we weren't far from your house! You

were supposed to find the slough on the map."

"Oh . . . that map." Chris rubs his face with his hand. "Um, yeah. I forgot to mention . . . "

"What?" A sneaky dread creeps up my throat.

"It sort of . . . fell in the fire . . . "

"What? Did it burn?"

Chris wrestles with his jacket and reaches into the pocket. He pulls out a limp and blackened piece of useless map. "The wind grabbed it."

"AUGH! Idiot!" I snatch the thing from his hand. Delicate ashes fall like butterflies from the corner and I can't even tell which corner it used to be. I feel dizzy. I take slow deep breaths but it doesn't help.

"Do you even know where we are?" I yell. "Do you recognize this slough?"

"I just moved here from Toronto four days ago. That was the first time I've even been out on my snowmobile."

"Toronto?" Of course, he's from a city. That explains a lot. "Then how could you know where we were going yesterday?"

The anger seethes through my clenched jaw. I don't even try to keep the panic out of my voice. Why does everything in my life get screwed up? The dogs raise their heads and study me.

"Well, I thought I knew . . . " Chris stumbles out of the sled. He stands in his boot liners with a purple goose egg on his forehead, crusted blood across his eyebrow below the bandage, and pink woollies that are four sizes too small.

He scratches his butt.

His forlorn expression tells me everything I need to know. This conversation is pointless and it's up to me and the dogs to get us home.

10

I STOMP AROUND CAMP, PREPARING for another day, and try to decide what to do next. As I see it, we have three options. We can just stay here and hope that we're found. I immediately reject this idea. There's no way I can sit still and wait for someone to help me.

We can go back the way we came. I think of all the new snow covering yesterday's tracks. Trying to follow our path through those ugly trails doesn't hold much appeal. But it's the known route—if we can find it, we probably should do that.

Or, we could continue this way. I stand, watching Whistler lick her paws with slow, methodical attention. If I remember the map right, the main trails are west of us. This trail we're on seems to be heading in that direction. If we find the main trails, we can follow them, and most likely cross a road. I'm sure of it. Lots of roads around here have dog team crossing traffic signs. And maybe heading west will be even faster than traveling the whole day backwards.

Or we could all freeze to death as we look for trails that aren't there. I finger the scar beside my ear, and feel a moment of regret over yesterday's decision to head north. I should have stuck to a trail I knew. Now I'm traveling blind out here. But I can't look back. Always moving forward—Dad's favorite saying.

Blue yodels softly at me and snaps me out of my

funk. I move closer to him, his butt swaying back and forth with fierce wagging.

"You think that's what we should do?" I ask, rubbing his cheek. "Keep moving forward? You remember Dad saying that, too?"

I blow out a slow breath and whisper, "I'm not sure what to do, Dad."

I swallow hard and remember Dad's confidence in Blue when he was still a yearling. I can almost hear him that day on the trapline.

"See what Blue is doing, Vic? How he's looking ahead past the leaders? You watch. He'll make a good leader someday."

The dogs had been breaking trail and we were plodding next to the sled to help lighten the load. The sled was full of wet beaver from the trapline, and the team worked hard through the deep snow. Blue pulled like a dog possessed, and peered ahead as if he wanted to see what was around the next corner.

We'd arrived home late that night, like so many

other times, and I was exhausted. And cranky. I wasn't much help, but Dad didn't mind. We tromped single file through the snow for the third trip unloading the sled, when he reached up and tapped the snow-laden branches hanging above us. Before I could catch myself, I walked right under it while the snow came down into my collar.

"Argh, Dad! Stop doing that!"

"Gotta keep you on your toes, Icky—whoa!"

I'd crashed into his knees to knock him over, but he stood rock solid. Always solid.

My chest feels hollow as the memory mows me over. *I don't have time for this. I have to get us home.*

"Forward it is, Blue. Good idea." The cold from the snow I'm kneeling in begins to seep through my leggings. Rocking back on my heels, I squeeze my eyes shut. I don't know if this is the right decision, I just know I have to find our way out soon. I think of the dog shed in the backyard full of frozen chicken and fat pallets, cooked rice, and vitamin packets. Fuel for working dogs. We can't spend another night out here; we have to get out today.

Once the dogs have been watered with the last of the chicken, we eat a breakfast of smoked sausage and a granola bar—the last of the food. It's still morning, but already I feel exhausted with worry. I can go hungry, and Chris can certainly starve to death for all I care, but my dogs cannot.

As we pack the sled, the silence between us could be cut in half with my hatchet. I grab our two water bottles that I refilled with boiled water from the slough, and stow them in the sled bag.

Chris jogs in place, bringing his knees up high, and then catches me staring at him. "This is not even cool," he says. "My jeans are so stiff, I can hardly move."

"If you weren't the biggest milquetoast loser I've ever met, I'd feel bad for you."

"Look, I'm sorry about the map, okay?" Chris glares down at me. "But who gives a map to someone who's sitting next to a fire? And it was so windy." He fingers his forehead, which reminds me I was going to check his gash. I gesture for him to bend closer so I can see it.

"You're supposed to be some sort of wilderness expert," he says. "Why don't you have a GPS like a normal—ow!" He straightens, holding his hand to his eyebrow after I rip off the bandage. "Hey!"

"Why do I need a GPS when I can read a map?" I snap back, gesturing again for him to bend closer. The lump over his eye is still red, but the dried blood around the gash makes it look worse than it is. I'm pleased the edges are closed. The bleeding seems to have stopped.

"Map reading is a skill anyone who comes out here should know," I continue. "Not like some people who prefer zooming around on some smelly machine thinking a little device will tell them where they are, batting their pretty eyes at whoever comes by." Absolutely not what I meant to say. At all.

Chris's mouth opens as if he's about to retort, but then closes. He looks at me with surprise. "Pretty eyes?"

"Pretty idiotic eyes, yeah."

"Think this will scar?" He strikes an exaggerated pose, blinking at me. I want to punch him.

"Chicks dig scars, right?"

"If you're going for some kind of freakish anime look, you've succeeded." I grab the sled and yank it onto the trail. "We need to go."

The dogs are pumped. They've been watching my every move and now that I've touched the sled, they leap to their feet. They scratch the ground and yawn with excitement when I look at them. They never complain. Never hold a grudge. Always trust.

I toss a harness to Chris. "Here, help me get the dogs ready. That's for Dorset, little brown girl on the end."

His amused expression turns to alarm. "I . . . I . . . don't know how."

"It's easy—just watch how I do it." I straddle Bean and hold up the harness. "See how I fold it at the double webbing? Yes, like that."

I slip it over Bean's head and the dog does the rest. Chris approaches Dorset as if she's a poisonous tarantula with Ebola virus. It's obvious he's afraid of dogs, but he still tries with the harness. I guess it's not his fault he's incompetent. But Dorset doesn't notice. She wags her tail furiously at his approach and it gives me a little warm feeling in the pit of my stomach.

I hook up Blue with Bean in lead. When I turn, I see Chris sliding toward the sled behind Dorset.

"Pick her front feet off the ground." I take her and hold the harness up so she's hopping on her back legs. "Shifts the four-wheel-drive down to two. Much easier."

As Chris struggles to harness Drift, I harness Gazoo and Whistler and hook them into the center of the gangline. They're in the team position. Drift and

Dorset, closest to the sled, are the wheel dogs. They tend to be the strongest dogs, though you wouldn't think it by looking at little Dorset. But if the sled gets stuck, they will both throw themselves into their harnesses and rapidly pop their tuglines until the sled is free. Drift, my crazy little tornado, is already lunging forward as I clip her in.

Frozen hard circles where the dogs had slept create icy dents that look like a plastic egg carton. I can tell which circle was Bean's; his metabolism cranks out so much energy he'd sink to China if we stayed here long enough. I worry about his weight, and wish I had brought extra fat for him.

I wind up the picket line and store it back in the sled, then step on the brake and motion for Chris to get in. The dogs' frantic screams ignite the air around us. Chris spastically trips and falls into the sled.

"Ready? All right!" We charge down the trail for about thirty yards and then it becomes obvious our travel today will be slow. The snow from yesterday's blizzard is so deep, the dogs have to jump like weasels. And the trail is really only a vague indent. I should've known this, but I was too busy showing off for Chris to think about it. I'll be glad when I drop this guy off at his house.

11

I STOP THE TEAM. "YOU'RE TOO HEAVY. Get out of the sled and help me back here."

"I'd rather not." But he climbs out and stands beside me. His face is tight and I feel a twinge of remorse for snapping at him. He seems defenseless, scared.

"What do I do?"

"You stand on that runner. I'll stand on this one. Hold on to the handlebar . . . it's like skiing, but you get to hang on." I have to yell above the dogs' frustrated barks. They don't like to stop when they've just started. I pull the hook again. "All right, Beanie!"

Chris looks frozen with fear, but after a few moments of smooth riding, his easy charm returns and he flashes me a wide grin. "Hey, this is fun."

"For now. They'll slow down soon and we'll have to pedal with one foot, or run beside the sled."

In fact, for most of the morning, no one is running. We plod through the snow, climb over broken and uprooted trees, and jockey the sled around tight corners. I keep hoping that around the next corner, the trail will widen out and I'll recognize where we are. But around each corner is more tangled mess and I curse my luck.

This has to be the thickest brush in Alaska. I sincerely wish we lived in an area that has cell coverage. With that thought, another rushes in.

Mom.

She's got to be freaking with the dogs and me not coming home last night. She'll know I'm out, but she won't know *where*.

The more I think about it, the more ill I feel imagining her at home alone. My heart aches as I recall a year ago last January. When we both sat at home — waiting. I think of her fragile show of cheerfulness, how it could buckle with this added pressure. She probably got home last night tired, expecting dinner. She would have been annoyed at first, then, as it got later, the cold dread would have crept in. I blink several times. Even with the anger that has boiled in my gut for over a year, I still don't want to see her hurt.

But I would never forgive her.

After Dad died, I heard her talking to Nana on the phone. She kept her voice low but I avoided the squeaky spot on the floor and crept close to her room. That's how I know Nana was trying to convince her to move back to Seattle. Mom used to be a city girl before she met Dad at a course they both took in the city.

Dad liked to improve his mind, always reading books and taking classes. He was probably the smartest fishing guide in Alaska. He convinced Mom she could work as a real estate agent in Spruce River, since he obviously couldn't trap or guide in the city. I don't think Nana ever let go of her grudge over that. Grandpa died years ago, and she's alone down there.

Mom hasn't really loved Alaska. Not like Dad and I do. I've been to the city to visit so I can tell it's not the place for me. Too many people, too much noise, too many cars on the roads. Not enough dog trails.

"You think we're close?" Chris asks, breaking me out of my thoughts.

"Yeah, we've got to cross a road eventually. Unless we get to your place first. Let me know if you see anything familiar."

We're on a slight downhill and the dogs pick up a little speed. Chris and I can both hop on the runners and ride. I make a show of digging in on one side of my runner and pulling the handlebar to steer the sled over to one side of the trail. I can't help stealing a glance to see if Chris is watching but he's busy gawking at the trees.

"Everything looks the same to me here. I used to live downtown on Bloor Street, surrounded by sidewalks and buildings. I've never seen this much snow in my life."

"You live in Canada and you're not used to snow? What kind of Canadian are you, eh?"

"She jokes!" Chris slaps his thigh with mock laughter. "Why do all Americans think we say 'eh' all the time? That's so lame. And I'm from *Toronto*. We don't get much snow. Our winters are just cold."

"I'm an *Alaskan*—so don't clump me with 'all Americans' or confuse me with some New Yorker you might know."

"Well, at least where I'm from you could tell by the stores where you were. Or just look at the street signs. Or hop on a streetcar. I'd give anything right now for a streetcar."

"I've never been on a streetcar."

The dogs are running faster, but I hardly take notice.

"You've never . . . Wow. Okay, they run on rails cut into the pavement and travel at about this speed. You usually have to stand and get bounced around kinda like this, too. But they're warmer. Oh, the warmth. Then we could hop off and hit a Tim Horton's. I'd kill for a Timmy's. And a cruller."

"A what? You mean *crul*-ler. It's pronounced with a short *u*."

Chris glances at me. "You don't have many friends, do you?"

I repress the urge to kick him. "Why did you . . . " I begin, but before I can react, the dogs completely disappear over a ridge.

I snap to attention, but too late to do anything but brace myself.

The sled launches over a dropoff that's at least as tall as I am. The dogs run low to the ground in a full sprint. The bottom falls out of my guts as we go airborne. I grip the handlebar even tighter when the sled tips sideways.

Chris screams as he flies off.

All I can do is hang on until the sled hits the ground. And when we hit, it knocks the wind out of my lungs. I hear an awful crunch. We continue plowing down the trail. The dogs drag the tipped-over sled with me still clinging to it, gasping for air. I'm sliding over the trail on my stomach. With one hand I reach for the brake while I clamp down on the stanchion with my other. I force the brake down, straining my arm with the effort. It takes a few moments for the dogs to slow down, but the sled finally stops.

12.

"Whoa! Whoa, Bean, whoa." I'm afraid to stand. If I've broken something, I don't want to know. I gingerly push up from the ground and test my legs. Everything seems to be working. Chris runs up behind me.

"Are the dogs okay?"

Now he's worried about the dogs. "Yeah, they

stayed on the ground. That was fun for them. I'm good, too, thanks for asking."

When I bend to pull the sled upright I notice Mr. Minky is dangling at an awkward angle like a loose tooth. The solid ash handlebar between the upright stanchions has split in two.

"Oh, no!" This was Dad's favorite of all the sleds he had made. I watched him build it. He shaped the runners and brush bow with steam and then pounded them into the molds. I'd sat cross-legged on his workbench and handed him tools. I was also in charge of keeping the wood stove going so the workshop stayed warm. Dad explained every stage to me as if I was another adult musher learning to build my own sled. My throat tightens.

Stupid, stupid. I should've paid more attention.

Chris inspects the two ends and pushes them together as if they'll magically meld. "Can you fix this?"

Pull it together, Victoria. You can fix this. "Of course."

I glance around at the saplings near the trail.

"What is this thing?" Chris pulls at Mr. Minky and I slap his hand away.

"None of your business."

The dogs roll in the snow as I kick the snow hook in, then pull out my hatchet.

"We'll splint it together with a couple of alders," I say. "I've got some duct tape in the sled bag. Can you find it?"

I spy two perfect saplings. After I cut them to length, I take off my mitts and use my fingers to hold the wood in place. The cold immediately attacks my exposed skin at the ends of my fingerless gloves. Chris finds the tape and stands next to me. I place the two pieces on either side of the broken handlebar.

"Tape it here," I say, and point with my chin.

"Say 'please.'"

"What?"

"I'll do it if you remember your manners. You have to say 'please.'"

"Chris, I swear to—"

"Okay, okay. Hostility!" He begins to whistle as he winds the tape around.

"Tape it all the way across so it's sturdy."

Chris's bent head is so close to mine, our frozen breath mingles and rises up as one cloud.

"This tape is strong. Like you could tie up a person with this stuff."

My blood freezes. "What?"

"I'm just saying . . . this is what they use in movies. It might work on the sled. Think it will hold?"

"I know it will." I try to ignore the unease of what he just said. Why would he be thinking of tying someone up?

"I've done this before when my dad broke his old sled. Well, I watched him do it. This will hold until we get back." I pull on my mitts and stow the hatchet deep in the sled bag. I glance at Chris.

Chris indicates behind us. "It's like someone came along with a backhoe here and dug out a rippin' hole in the trail."

"Yeah, it must've been a mudslide," I say. "Anyway, you have to stay on the sled. If you fall off again, I'm not coming back for you."

I enjoy the image in my mind of waving goodbye to him as he lies on the trail.

"Did you see my lift-off?" Chris sweeps his hand in an arc. "Cra-zy. I got serious air."

I muffle a snicker then refocus on the sled. It's about time to start using my head. I pull out my snowshoes from the bag.

"We should all take turns breaking trail." I slip my mukluks into the bindings and then shuffle toward the leaders. Bean groans as I rub his ears. "Good boy."

He grins at me with his tongue hanging as if he's having the time of his life.

Sometimes I wish I could trade places with the dogs. They only have to worry about running and eating. They love fiercely and don't worry about things they can't control. And when someone dies, they can sit on top of their house, throw their head back, and howl. Then they can begin a new day.

I stomp into the fresh snow in front of the lead dogs and they both step on my shoes.

"You have to ride the brake!" I turn to see Chris clutching the handlebar with a steel grip. His round eyes are studying the wheel dogs.

"Well, I don't know how to do this," he yells.

"I'm not going as fast as they are. Just don't let the leaders run me over." How did I let myself get into this situation? Alone out here with a guy I don't know anything about. And one who obviously doesn't know anything about the outdoors.

I think of last night and how his body had been wrapped around mine and the pit of my belly feels warm. Sarah would flip if she knew. She's totally into guys, and they're into her, too. Which makes sense because the Athabascan side of her gene pool gifted her with stunning looks. With her long, silky straight hair that shines like a pelt around her perfect tawny skin that seems to glow from within, and deep brown eyes, she can have any guy she wants. And she's always going out with someone. As if she doesn't want to be alone, which is dumb since she has me. And about four thousand brothers, sisters, aunts, and uncles. I'm so jealous of her big family. I think I first started hanging out with her so I could go over to her house and sit in the middle of all that chaotic noise and energy. Especially when her older brother dropped in with his dog team. Sarah kept teasing me because she thought I had a crush on him. As if. It was the dogs I was interested in.

But her interests are more southern. As soon as we graduate, she's gone to California. Her dream. She dresses as if she lives there already, which is another reason guys like her. She is a fun, loud, and wild center of attention, and hard to resist.

It's not as if I've never gone out with anyone. I grimace thinking of my short and tragic past with Randy Fuller. Maybe I felt sorry for him. Maybe he wore Bart Simpson T-shirts every day because his development was stunted. Back in grade school, he fell asleep at Mark Hamilton's birthday party, and they super-glued his finger to the inside of his nostril. That kind of humiliation is hard to get past in a small town. So in eighth grade I called myself his girlfriend. I even let him hold my hand in the school hall. I shake my head at the memory. It feels like a lifetime ago, even though it was only last year.

We're moving through a stunted black spruce stand. It crowds in thicker and thicker, which tells me it hasn't been maintained in a long time. Which means we've gone seriously wrong with choosing to go this way. No self-respecting trapper would use this trail, so it's highly unlikely we'll run into anyone messing around in here.

Soon, I hardly see a path through the coarse branches. They twist and grab at us as we go by. My hair snags on a branch. Sharp needles rake my cheek. I take another step and my hat gets knocked off.

I'm bent over holding up a long branch for the dogs to come through, when I hear a droning noise.

"A helicopter!" I yell to Chris.

He looks up. Black spruce branches tangle together above our heads with a few little windows of overcast sky between them. The chopper blades beat the cold air with a staccato that echoes in my ears. But when I glimpse it, it is farther away than it sounds. We both jump up and down waving our arms as much as we can within the scrubby bush.

"HERE!" I scream.

"HEY!" Chris yells. "We're right here!"

Look down, look down, look down, look down. Are they seeing us? My pulse races. *Please, see us.* We could be home.

With food.

Safe.

The dogs safe. I could stop being responsible for everyone.

My heart pounds, then deflates when the helicopter continues on its way.

"If we can't see them, they can't see us." The disappointment is so bitter, I almost choke trying to swallow the lump.

"NO! No, no, no, no." Chris covers his head with his arms, then savagely kicks at the snow and falls to his knees.

"They were so close," he rages. He pounds his fists into the snow. "Why didn't we just stay in the open field? They would've seen us then!"

I feel a quick pain as if I've been jabbed in the stomach. *He's probably right.*

Since we left the swamp, we've followed the narrow trappers' trails that are overgrown and hidden. No one will see our tracks from the air. Even our tracks from this morning will probably just look like a pack of wolves had been there.

We've gone so far now we can't turn back even

if we wanted to. I highly doubt I'd be able to find the trail. We can only keep going. But how far? We could be out here for days before we cross a road. I imagine all the wide green space on the topo map. *What if we are going the wrong way?*

An icy dread runs through me. We could all die out here running straight through to nowhere. If I could just study my map one more time.

"If we had a map, then we wouldn't be here, would we?"

"If we had a GPS, then we'd be home eating cheeseburgers," Chris barks back. I can see the fire in his eyes from here. "Or if we had snowmobiles, instead of these stupid dogs!"

I suck in my breath as if he's slapped me. I'm about to scream back, but then his expression reveals the fear he's been hiding.

Chris quickly rubs his face with both hands. A silent moment stretches between us. The only sounds are the constant wind moaning through the tree branches and the dogs grunting with contentment as they scratch their backs in the snow.

Chris clasps his hands behind his neck. "Forget it," he says with a much softer voice. He hauls himself to his feet, brushing the snow off his jeans. "I'm just mad."

I'm mad, too. At myself, at him, at this whole situation. But I can't help myself as I point to his jeans. "Try not to roll around in the snow with those. The woollies underneath will only do so much to keep you warm."

He gapes at me, then snorts, adjusting his scarf and shaking his head with a bemused expression.

I bend to hug Bean. His hot tongue brings me back to center, and after a moment I feel ready to stand.

"Okay. Anyway. Let's keep going out of this nasty spot at least. We'll find the main trails soon. No point sitting here crying."

"Hope we find a Tim Horton's soon, too," Chris says.

13

THE COLD, DARK PART OF EVENING arrived suddenly. Like entering the haunted house my town sets up at Halloween. Your eyes struggle to adjust from the daylight to the oppressive darkness of the interior, strain to see the scary things before they jump out at you.

But I didn't have to see the scary things to know

they were here. Scary things like dehydration. Starvation. Hypothermia. Scary like the skin on Bean's shoulders sticking up for a second when I pinch it — the first sign of dehydration. Scary like sleeping another night in the sled bag with Chris.

"Whoa," Chris says in my ear. His arms are around me in the nest of the bag and we both hear the loud complaining of his stomach. I actually feel it on my back. "It's rebelling after that tea."

Without food, our bodies are having a harder time staying warm. And tonight is much colder than last night. It's hard to guess how cold because I haven't eaten so I'm feeling it more than usual. Even the furnace that is Chris's body is barely radiating the BTUs it did last night.

Go hungry — get cold.

I thought about making a proper lean-to shelter to reflect back the heat of the fire, but that seemed like so much work. All of our energy should be used to move forward and get ourselves out to a road. We couldn't afford to waste any time or effort making a shelter when we already had one. I shiver again and feel Chris's arms tighten.

We've set camp near another slough. Plenty of water, but the dogs didn't drink enough for the energy they are putting out. And they're used to baited water. I still don't recognize the land or the slough, but I'm guessing, since we haven't come to a road or main trail, that we've somehow gotten turned around far north of where I wanted to be. Without a map, my compass doesn't tell us much. I don't need a compass to show where west is when I have the sun.

Calculations buzz in my head. If we've been out here two days, possibly traveling twenty miles a day with this deep snow and slow speed, we definitely should have crossed Cook's road by now. Maybe we're running parallel to it.

I'd scraped the inner bark from a birch and tried eating it. Dad told me once it could be used as emergency food because it's starchy. But I guess I was thinking of potatoes when I heard starch. It was nothing like potatoes. Sort of like eating sawdust, and it was so bitter, it made my eyes water.

But I boiled some white birch twigs in a dog dish for us, and that had been okay. Slightly sweet. And nice to have something warm inside my stomach. The fact that I had just been joking the night before about eating yellow birch twigs hadn't escaped me. I never thought we'd be out here so long.

I had eyed the beaver house on the bend in the slough and sorely wished that I'd brought snares. With snares, we could trap beaver. Or rabbits—though the meat wouldn't be as rich. I could have set the snares overnight, and perhaps gone to sleep with the knowledge we'd be fed in the morning. That the dogs would be fed.

I did not bring snares, however. And I'm certain the gnawing guilt and worry are going to keep me awake most of the night. I try to imagine what Dad would do, but that makes me feel worse because I know Dad would have brought snares. Besides the tea, what else can we eat out here? And we must eat. No fuel in the furnace, no life.

"Every time I close my eyes I see a stuffed crust pizza with ham and pineapple." Chris's voice breaks through the dark.

"Pineapple on pizza? That's not right."

Chris chuckles. "What's the first thing you're gonna eat, Secret? When we get back."

I don't want to say out loud my first thought —that we might not get back at all. So I play along. "Um. Maybe spaghetti with thick moose-meat sauce and mushrooms."

"Oh, that's boring."

"Well, how about some of those Christmas oranges? Juicy and sweet, with no pits. And the pajamas peeled off them."

"Pajamas?"

"You know, the white stuff under the skin. That's got to go."

"Too healthy. I'm going to eat a couple of Big Macs, then a chocolate shake. Then a whole pan of brownies . . . maybe topped with some raw cookie dough. Oh, and blueberry pancakes! I make those a lot at home. With gobs of syrup and strawberry sauce. And bacon, fried crispy. Some scrambled eggs and cheese — cooked so they're not runny. I can't stand runny eggs." Chris's voice strains at the edge of a whisper in his excitement about food. What is it about the dark that makes people whisper?

"Actually," Chris says, "I wouldn't even mind if they were runny."

Chris's appetite is not satisfied until he's described every meal he's ever cooked, eaten, or thought about eating.

"You know, you're going to be disappointed in Spruce River. The only place to eat is the coffee shop and I wouldn't recommend it. You have to drive over an hour to get to McDonald's, even."

"Well, I guess I'll just cook more. I like to cook."

"Why did you guys move anyway? What does your dad do?"

Chris pauses for a moment and we lie still, the silence hanging between us in the darkness. "He didn't come with us. They split a few years ago."

"Oh. Sorry."

"That's okay. Mom got transferred at her insurance firm. She must've really screwed up at work."

"How can your mom work here? Wouldn't she need like a green card or something?"

"She's originally from Boston, but moved to Canada before I was born. She met my dad in Toronto."

"Is he still in Toronto then?"

"Yeah, I'll be going back to visit."

"When do you —" An eerie howl interrupts me. It bursts out from the north, behind where the dogs are staked out. And it sounds close.

"What — ?" Chris gasps in my ear. An answering howl rises up again. With many voices.

"Wolves," I tell him.

"I know it's wolves," Chris hisses. "I've heard them on TV. But it's so different when they're *live*. Actually right *there* in the dark."

Chris shuffles and his knee jabs me in the ribs. "Whoa, my arm hairs are standing up! Man that's spooky. They sound like they're right in camp."

The dogs rustle nervously outside so I push aside the flap on the sled bag and sit up. Freezing air attacks me. Once I'm out of the dimness of the canvas bag, I see the cloudless night sky lighting our campsite with the glow from the stars and half a moon. The hairs in my nostrils stiffen as I inhale.

I see the outlines of all six dogs nestled in a row beside us, but I shine my headlight at them to make sure they're okay. Their eyes glow back at me. I point the light into the gloom around us, half expecting to see many more shining eyes, but there is nothing. The howling ends abruptly and once again it's dead quiet except for the cracking trees.

The embers from the fire are comforting. I wish

I could toss more wood on from here, but I'm already shivering again. I scoot back into the bag, shutting off the light, and close the top flap.

"That's the wild letting us know it isn't sleeping."

"Huh?"

"We have to be aware of things all the time. Respect it. Maybe the wolves are just passing through," I say loudly. "We should make noise to let them know we're here."

Chris bursts into singing at the top of his voice. "There was an old lady who swallowed a fly. I don't know why, she swallowed the fly . . . "

I endure another few minutes of Chris's camp-fire songs before he winds down. The dogs have settled now, too. As if the singing comforted them. The thought warms my insides.

"I used to sing all the time when I was younger," Chris says. "My buddy Cam and I even talked about starting a band. I play guitar, he plays drums. I used to go to his apartment sometimes on the weekends and we'd play video games and practice for our future stardom as musicians."

Chris shifts slightly to his right, which means I have to shift, too. We both uncurl then curl like two dragonflies in a hard wind.

"He had the tallest bunk beds I've ever slept in. The top bunk was his older brother's, but he moved out. So when I stayed over, that's where I slept. I'm not cool with heights, but I never told him that. Just climbed up to the top of those beds.

"Then one night I woke from a bad dream. I jumped up and the ceiling fan got me in the head. I still have the scar."

Chris grabs my hand in the dark and guides it to his forehead. I touch a small, thin bump along his hairline that I hadn't noticed before. I feel along the ridges for a moment longer than I need to, and suddenly drop my hand.

"Yeah, nice scar."

I briefly think of telling him about the time I

took three dogs with my bike. I had wanted to try Bean in lead. But for some crazy reason, I decided it'd be even more fun with Drift and Gazoo. The first three minutes were the wildest of my life. We tore out of the yard while I perched on the bike with a death grip and wide eyes. The rest of the time I spent on my face dragging along the dirt road. By the time I got them back to the house, my coveralls were ripped to shreds, and I was covered in mud and blood. I still have the scars running down the left side of my belly. Heat creeps up my neck as I think of showing that to Chris.

"I've got one here." I surprise myself by sticking my hand in Chris's to show him my index finger. His warm fingers run over mine as he searches for my scar.

"When I was young, I was feeding peanuts to a squirrel in our backyard. I guess he thought my finger was a peanut because he grabbed it, then his mouth got stuck or something 'cause he just hung on while I flung my hand around."

"And that's why I prefer the indoors." Chris touches the jagged bump beside my nail.

"I was screaming and crying and the thing finally flew off. He was probably mentally scarred for life."

"You're worried about the squirrel? That's rich. He probably gave you rabies or something. Did you get checked?"

"No, no. I don't have rabies, I'm just a carrier. Whatever you do, don't touch me or you'll get it."

The hunger and stress must be taking a toll on my good judgment for me to enjoy bantering like this with Chris in the dark. Actually, it's because it's dark that I'm doing it. In the morning, I'll probably feel embarrassed to look at him. I flip back and forth, berating myself and secretly grinning until restless sleep finally claims me.

My eyes open again before daylight, not knowing what woke me. I listen intently but don't hear any more wolves. Then Chris murmurs in his sleep. "Hide . . . come on . . . the wolf . . . run!"

I lie still, trying to ignore the cramps in my belly. After a few seconds of silence, I let out my breath. Chris is quiet again, breathing slow and heavy. I listen to the rhythm of it, pondering the mystery of him. Of how I behave when I'm with him.

I have a bad taste in my mouth from not brushing for two days. I put my hand in front of my face and breathe into it to check my breath. I'll chew the end of a slender green sapling when we get up and brush the scum from my teeth. And maybe wash with warm water. It will help me feel better. Yes. Today, we're going to find a road.

Just because we're out here doesn't mean we should be dirty and unkempt. Another of Dad's proverbs. He made sure we were as clean and presentable out here as we were at home. "You can tell a good bushman from how comfortable he keeps himself. Or herself," he'd say with a wink.

We'd wash up right from the river, or heat the water and I'd hold the compass mirror up so Dad could shave. If there wasn't any water, we'd use snow. I love the way my skin feels after a fresh snow bath. I grin imagining it, but then the familiar ache rushes through me so fast, I gasp. How could I have known that soon, he'd be gone, and all that grace would disappear from the earth?

"Dad," I whisper. "Could use a little help."

14

TUESDAY

AFTER A BREAKFAST OF MORE BIRCH twig tea that only makes me hungrier, I fill our water bottles with the rest of the tea for later.

The dogs look at me expectantly. They grab my heart and squeeze. My eyes burn from the shame of getting them into this situation.

"I'm sorry, girl," I say softly to Dorset. "I don't have anything for you this morning."

Her foxlike face is tipped in frost, and she hasn't even uncurled from her bed. She's trying to conserve her heat. The jacket isn't enough if she's not eating. *How much longer could they hold on?*

When we head down the trail again, Chris and I each ride on a runner. I feel sluggish. Normally my stance is secure and solid on the back of the sled, whether I'm riding one runner or two. Now I feel unbalanced on weak legs. I spent too long jogging in place trying to warm up, and I'm light-headed. My insides are hollow. A shiver of fear mixes with my shaking from the cold.

I think back to when I decided to go on this trip. It seems like weeks ago now. *Stupid, stupid.* I glower at Chris out of the corner of my eye. It occurs to me that if I'd crossed to the trail at a different spot, I may have missed him altogether. The anger helps cover the guilt so I follow that thought.

Idiot guys from Toronto think they can ride a snow-mobile along a trail and not know where they're going or what they should wear so they don't get hypothermia and put someone else's life in danger, then pretend they actually know where they are—

I catch a glimpse of movement out of the corner of my eye and look up. Several ravens are circling low over a stand of white spruce ahead and my breath catches. Their glossy black feathers shine in the sun, making them radiant in flight.

"Look!" I raise a hand, shielding my eyes. "Ravens!" Hope flutters in my belly.

"Yeah. So?"

Now I hear their cackling calls. Just past that granite outcrop. The trail runs along the side of the rock. I stop the team and a raven sitting in the lower spruce branches takes off, cawing loudly.

"So just stay here with the dogs." I grab the snowshoes and jump off the trail. I scramble and claw my way up the hill, not even caring if I get sweaty or my clothes get damp. My heart pounds. The loose snow pills on the surface behind me. It rolls and skitters down the top crust. When I crest the ridge, I look down into a clearing and let out a huge breath.

The clearing looks like a war was waged here. Trampled snow stretches from the rock to the tree line, as if the site had been cleared for a party. Scrubby willows are bent down, young poplar snapped off. Blood and hair litter the scene.

But the best thing about it is the moose.

A freshly killed moose, mostly eaten, lies on its side in the snow. Even from here I can tell that the front shoulder is almost untouched beneath it, and the head is still intact.

I raise my arms in the air and whoop. *Thank you, Dad! Thank you, wolves.*

"What? What do you see? Is it a road?"

I turn and smile down at Chris. "How do you feel about McMoose for breakfast?"

Dawning comprehension flashes across his face and he grins back, giving me two thumbs-up.

For the next few hours, we work together. Chris is learning how to start a fire and stake out the dogs. I use my hatchet to hack, shave, and saw off pieces of meat from the shoulder and the neck. I pick away at the carcass just like one of those ravens, or a turkey vulture. Little nips, pulls, tears.

The dogs get most of it, chunks of about two pounds each. When I give it to them, I cannot describe the joy it brings me. My whole body vibrates with emotion. I fight back tears.

The dogs gnaw rib bones that I've managed to crack off while I wait for the meat scraps and bone chips to boil. This will give them some nice meaty broth to drink.

"It's really too bad I can't get at the nutrition inside the skull," I say to Chris as I slice. "It's way too big to try to boil in a dish. And to sever it, I would need something better than my hatchet."

"Mmm. Brraaiins." Chris pats his stomach. He breaks a dead spruce branch and places it on the fire. It flares up.

I cube the rest of the meat for us and throw the pieces into the other dog dish with boiling water. Chris stares at it with eyes so full of yearning, I forgive him for his earlier comments on my "cruel" lifestyle of eating animals that we've hunted. Just where did he think the meat came from all wrapped up in the grocery stores? Maybe he'll understand once he's lived here a little longer.

The moose had been a bull, an old bull by the looks of his worn teeth. The boiled meat is rubbery and tough to chew.

I've never tasted anything so delicious.

I scald my lips on the broth in my eagerness. When the food goes down, I can almost feel the warmth and energy seeping into my arms and legs.

"Mmm, oh, nomph, this is *so* good!" Chris closes his eyes while he takes a turn at slurping from the bowl. He fishes out another chunk and chews. When I take the bowl back, we look at each other over this shared victory and grin with shiny lips.

We eat all that we can salvage. I can't break off any more of the larger bones to bring with us, and all the edible parts are gone. It's not enough, but a definite improvement from before. I decide to let the dogs rest a little.

"If you like moose meat, you'll love the feasts at the community center. Especially the Christmas one." I sit back on top of the sun-warmed sled bag and let out a big sigh. Chris drapes his tall body against a rock and nods.

"Hard to imagine eating with a whole community. But sounds cool." He tilts his face toward the sun.

"We have feasts all the time, but the Christmas one is always special. When I was little, my parents would wrap me up in the dogsled and we'd all go. I was in charge of holding Dad's guitar. I remember coming 'round the last corner on the trail and

135

seeing all the red and green lights they put on the tree in front of the hall. We'd stake the team outside and then walk through the front doors into a wall of heat and baking smells. Mrs. Charlie's moose-meat pie, Mr. Wicker's moose-ball stew, roast moose, sweet and sour moose, and for dessert there'd be chocolate mousse. That's where I first tasted jungle berry juice. I thought it was the best thing ever. I pleaded with my mom to put it in my lunch, but she didn't know what I was talking about.

"'I can't find jungle berry juice anywhere. I don't know what it is,' she had said. So I had to do my own investigating. Turns out, it was just milk with strawberry syrup. But I still like it."

"Hey, I've had that! It's good!"

"I know, right? Anyway, there was another tree decorated with lights inside, too. All the kids would get gifts from Santa and we'd play games. Then Dad would unwrap his guitar and play songs that everyone could sing along with. My favorite was 'Cat Came

Back.' I'd sing the chorus the loudest. But, now that I think about it, that song is sort of evil with what the poor cat goes through. I just liked it 'cause I was cheering for him.

"Then, at the end of the party, we'd go back outside to the team and it was always freezing cold compared to the heat of the hall. When the dogs took us down the trail, and we'd go past the reach of the lights, it was like traveling into another world. So quiet and dark and adventurous. But I could never stay awake for the ride home. I always woke up the next day in my bed."

I'm astonished at myself for talking so much. Chris watches me with a thoughtful expression. His eyes, squinting against the sun, seem lit up. The ends of his brown hair dance in the breeze, the curls sticking out from the bottom of the scarf he now regularly wears as a hat.

I clear my throat, a little embarrassed. "The dogs have rested. We should get moving."

A slow grin spreads across his face as he continues to watch me with that peculiar look. Then he pushes off from his rock and adjusts his scarf. "I was just getting comfortable here."

I start breaking trail with snowshoes even though the trail is already broken with all the animal tracks running along it.

"What are all these tracks from?" Chris asks.

"The trail system makes handy routes for wildlife out here. The trails get animals out of the deep snow and thick brush. So they also make good hunting corridors."

I notice the tall spruce lining this section of trail and wonder if we'll see any marten, with their cute little round ears and sweet faces. I'd like to show Chris a marten just to see the look on his face.

Our travel is painfully slow. At this rate, from all the time spent making fires, boiling water, cleaning moose, not to mention moving through deep snow, we should make it out by spring.

15

THE DOGS SEEM HAPPIER. I FEEL their enthusiasm behind me as I plod along. I'm very careful not to work up a sweat and get damp, so I stop often.

There has been little wind since the storm. The trees are still. It's so peaceful out here when it's quiet like this. I could almost forget we're lost and starving. With the sun out, I imagine how wonderful it will be in a few weeks. Dad always played a game every year waiting for spring. "You can hear it breaking the back of winter," he'd say.

When I was young, I took this literally, and tried listening for some kind of spine-snapping noises. Once, we heard the creek ice let go with a loud crack that echoed across the valley, and I was convinced that was winter's back.

The dogs pant behind me, and the snow makes little shushes as I shuffle in my snowshoes. Around us, the arched limbs of alder and birch take turns losing their snow loads with a soft *whoomp*. They spring upward, free of their burdens.

"So do all mushers run six dogs in a team?" Chris asks behind me.

"No, no. That's just how many I brought along for this trip. I have sixteen. It all depends on what you're doing, how much weight you have in the sled, how far you're going, what the trail conditions are like."

I keep moving in front of the team, but turn my head so Chris can hear me. "The main thing is not to have too many and be overpowered. That's dangerous for everyone."

"Huh. I guess you don't need many dogs to pull you."

I glance back with a mock offended expression.

He doesn't know how true his words are. Two years ago, I had too many dogs on a run. Of course, I had waited till Dad wasn't around, then hooked up a ten-dog team. That was a wild ride. I thought I was so cool running that long string of dogs all by myself. Fun—until we got to the road where I couldn't sink the snow hook. Instead of going straight across the road and onto the trail, Beetle, the little tramp, had veered into a ditch to get to the village dog that was walking loose near the trees.

We crashed, or, more to the point, I crashed, and watched my whole team take off down the road without me, dragging the broken sled. I had limped up the driveway of the nearest house, which turned out to be Noel Chambers's place, and he proceeded to tell the whole school what a complete noob I was, and worse, that I was a bad musher. And his dad had to take me on his snowmobile about a mile to the next homestead just in time to watch Beetle tie with the male dog and a fight erupt in the team. Mr. Chambers helped me break up the fight while I pretended not to notice the two dogs caught in a canine version of wanton lust, which was pretty hard since Beetle was squealing like a vixen. I usually run smaller teams now since I don't need to repeat that kind of drama.

"The dogs are always looking at you, you know?" Chris says. "Like they're connected to you. It's cool."

My face flushes immediately and I bite back a smile. It surprises me that he'd notice something like that.

"The dogs are reading me for how they're supposed to react to something. It's important to stay calm so they don't freak out. They look at my face, but also my posture, how I'm holding myself, the tone of my voice—all of it." As I explain, I straighten my shoulders back a bit more and dart a glance to Chris. For the first time, I wonder if he's trying to read me as well.

"You think they're looking at me, too?"

"Yes, that's how they communicate."

"Must make you tired," Chris says, "trying to stay calm for the dogs all the time."

We don't speak for a few paces as I keep the rhythm of my steps in the snow.

Chris breaks the silence. "You want me to take a turn up front?"

I glance around, surprised to realize I've been trudging along for quite a distance. We won't make this kind of time with Chris in lead I bet.

"Have you ever been on snowsh—"

The dogs' screams interrupt me. "Yes, Bean, we're going."

I turn to start moving again just as I hear a

different kind of scream—high-pitched and distinctly girly. It's Chris.

"Look out!"

Then I see it. A huge cow moose is coming around the corner of the trail directly at us. She stops at the noise of the dogs, swivels her ears, blows snot out her nose, and stares at us. She's standing in the middle of the trail about three team-lengths away. Fifteen hundred pounds of unpredictable animal with razor-sharp hooves.

Blood hammers down my arms leaving my elbows feeling as if they aren't part of my body. All moisture leaves my mouth. My legs feel rooted to the trail and for an awful second, all I see is black. She won't give up the trail. With her long, narrow legs, she'll sink in the new snow. Behind me, the dogs shove into my legs and I snap out of my panic.

"Git!" I scream. I wave my hands above my head to look bigger. "Go on! GET OFF THE TRAIL!" My heart pounds. This can't be happening.

The moose sways a little on the trail as if indecisive. I yell louder and stomp my feet. She looks behind her. Seems to think about it. Then she puts her head down and charges toward us.

I let out a scream, but she keeps steaming toward us like a train on a track. She's charging at a gallop, and it's as if I'm watching her in slow motion. Time has slowed down to a crawl. I see frost blowing from her nose like a steam engine. The trail shakes from her thundering hooves. She's so big. I can even smell her. Pungent. Horsey.

"Look OUT!" I hear again behind me.

I don't think—just bend down and yank off a snowshoe. When I stand, she is less than ten paces from us. Bearing down. The dogs have gone quiet. My pulse roars in my ears. I fling the snowshoe as hard as I can. It flies through the air like a Frisbee. It hits her square in the face. The *thwack* sound is surprisingly loud in the cold air. She stops short. Her large brown eyes study us.

"Augh!" I scream, waving my arms.

And then she wheels around and charges back down the trail.

My knees buckle and I fall in the snow. The dogs break into a frenzy of barking in their desire to chase. Blue leaps over me with eagerness. I reach up from where I'm sitting and grab the gangline, digging my feet into the trail. I notice I've been holding my breath and I let it out in a whoosh. My heart hammers in my throat. I take off my other snowshoe with a shaking hand.

"Holy crap, holy crap." Chris is losing it behind the sled. He runs toward me, leaving the sled unattended.

The dogs explode forward, with me hanging on to the gangline. Suddenly, I'm yanked between the dogs, my arms stretched above my head, my hip dragging on the trail.

"Set the hook! The snow hook!" I grip the gangline with damp gloves, dig into the snow with my knees to slow us, and feel Gazoo's feet tramping me as he runs. The dogs are powerhouses when they want to be. The strength of a dog team can pull cars out of ditches. They can haul loads of firewood or pelts down narrow, twisting trails. A dog team on a mission can be like a runaway plow truck.

I glimpse Chris as he grabs for the sled.

And misses.

"Run!" I yell as snow fills my mouth. I roll on the trail feeling as if I'm speeding along in a dune buggy —only without the buggy. My internal organs are being rearranged by the pounding.

My hands slide down the gangline. I'm losing my grip. I frantically try to pull myself up. With my outstretched arms covering my ears, the sound of my own rapid breathing is all I hear. When I lift my head to see where we're going, I get a face full of snow and my grip slips farther. If I lose the team they'll keep running right toward that moose. They will not come back for us, won't stop because I've fallen off. They're trained to run straight down a trail. I can't let go.

The team pounds down the trail. I can hardly breathe with the snow clogging my nose, filling my mouth. My hands slip further.

Don't let go.

I'm dragging between endless legs, feet clawing up the trail, digging into my body. My fingers are frozen into hooks. I can't grab. Can't see. How far have we come? Where is the moose? We must be almost on her by now.

Don't let go.

I dig my knees in to slow us, but it just makes my grip slip another few inches. The sled bounces behind me. My feet kick it.

Don't let go!

I have to do something. Panic floods to the surface as if I'm drowning in it. Drowning in white, frozen desperation. I can't hold on much longer. My guts must be spread out behind us. I can't feel anything below my neck.

Slip.

Bounce.

Claw frantically.

Faster than a gasp, the sled runs me over and I'm face down alone on the trail.

I look up just in time to see the sled disappear around the next bend. Shakily, I sit up. I've lost my hat and snow is packed solidly up my sleeves, down my neck, up my nose. I'm starving. Alone in the winter bush. Wet.

And I've lost my dog team.

"Idiot!" My throat threatens to close and I realize with horror that I'm about to cry. *Get a grip.* I take deep breaths and try to think.

Must get the team. I lurch to my feet and take stock of all my limbs. Everything is still there. Melting snow drips down my back. My sleeves have jammed up to my elbows and my arms are red with freezer burn. My whole body feels as if I've gone through the rinse cycle. I'm probably black and blue underneath, but right now, I have to get my dogs.

I begin to jog with jerky steps, following the tracks the dogs have made.

The last time I lost the team, after our headlong charge through the ditch, the snow hook had knocked loose with the bouncing. It had embedded itself in the trail finally, too late to prevent Beetle from getting knocked up, but it had at least stopped the team. I can only hope that happens again. I think of the upright sled, sliding happily along. If only the sled fell over, it could slow the dogs down.

My heart races at the thought of the dogs facing that moose. Have they caught her? Please, don't let them be trampled.

I run, pump my legs as fast as I can manage. I don't care how much I sweat, I'm dead anyway if I don't find the team. The soft trail slows each of my footsteps, like running in a nightmare when you can't get anywhere. I finally make it around the corner, but the tracks keep going over the next ridge. Don't think. Just run. One foot, then the other. Keep moving.

Must get dogs. Must get dogs. I chant this as I run and it becomes the only thing I care about. Keep moving. Get the team.

I crest the ridge and still no sign. I stop to suck in wheezy breaths. The adrenaline is keeping me moving, but my energy tank is almost at zero.

Then I hear it. I hold my breath to listen, and my stomach feels as if I've just swallowed lead.

Faint, horrific screaming.

I bolt ahead and skirt around a white birch stand. Finally I see them.

The dogs are in a ball with Bean tangled in the middle. The gangline is wrapped around his front leg. Drift and Whistler are locked in battle—pulling the gangline tightly, pinching Bean. The other dogs have jumped him, egged on by his screams of pain. It's all so horrible that I can barely look.

"STOP!" I scream as I reach them. "Drift! Enough!" I bring my face down right beside the flashing teeth and scream into their faces. It makes them pause long enough for me to break them apart and start untangling.

The rest of the dogs seem to be coming out of a hypnotic trance. They blink at me and shoot dirty glances at each other. Dog fights always trigger their primal instincts. They take on a pack mentality and pick on whoever is losing. Thank goodness they hardly ever fight. They argue all the time, but what looks extreme to anyone who doesn't know them is just them sorting things out. They need to do that to avoid any serious fighting.

I have no idea what happened here. Did Bean try to turn around to find me? Did they catch up with the moose and then the fight started? I can't tell from the chaos of tracks.

"Bean, are you okay?" He sways on three legs, his left front leg held off the ground. His head hangs down.

My stomach squeezes as if it's been stabbed with an ice pick. I whip off my gloves and gingerly feel his leg. My hands tremble. I quickly find a nasty puncture wound on the top of his leg next to his elbow. This kind of injury is common in a dog fight. I clean it with snow, and spread his fur to get a better look. That's when I find the gash deep in his shoulder, which is far more ominous. Slowly, I extend his leg forward to check his range of motion, watching his reaction. He pulls away. My mouth goes dry. Did the moose kick him? If he has internal damage to his ligaments, there isn't much I can do. I follow the muscle from his elbow to the shoulder, and feel a tendon tremble against my finger. He needs a shoulder pack, which I do not have.

Gazoo has recovered from the fight and pops his tug to get going again.

"Shhh, it's okay, Gazoo. Settle down." If I keep my tone low, it calms the dogs.

Uncle Leonard tells me the more you pretend at being something, the closer you are to making it real. So just make sure you're pretending the right things.

It becomes a habit. Considering how often I act like I'm in control of everything in front of the dogs, I should be pretty close to it by now.

When I unhook Bean and gather him in my arms, he doesn't struggle or whimper. His bravery makes me want to be a better musher. One that doesn't put her dogs in danger, and has enough food to feed them.

Adrenaline must still be coursing through me because I pick up the fifty-pound dog even though I feel about as strong as a wet noodle. I manage to carry him back to the sled. My legs wobble as I set him inside the sled bag. I'm panting as I arrange the gear to make him comfortable. Once I've clipped his neckline to the handlebar, I pull out the first-aid kit.

There's a small roll of gauze left, and I grab that with the scissors. I quickly snip away the fur around the wounds, to see better and keep out contaminants. Bean watches but lies still until I probe his shoulder.

"Almost done, Bean."

Using snow to wash the blood, I wish I had a

larger kit with Betadine. I wipe blood away from the torn flesh. He has severe bruising under his fur, and the swelling has already started. Gathering a handful of clean snow, I pack it over the front point of his shoulder joint, then wrap the roll of gauze around to hold the makeshift ice pack in place. It's the last of the gauze, and it's just enough. I tape the end, then smooth the fur on Bean's muzzle.

When I straighten, I wipe my hot face with the back of my mitt, and take a deep breath before I look behind us. The trail is empty.

I'm going to have to go back for him.

16

It doesn't take us long to find Chris. Even from a distance I see his face is flushed from jogging. He stops when he sees us and collapses on his knees, hanging his head in his hands.

The dogs sprint forward with obvious joy, as if they've been looking everywhere for him, and now he's finally found.

As we get closer, Chris stands and yells, "Is everyone okay? Are you hurt?"

I stop the team and stomp on the hook as Chris jogs to greet us. His gaze bounces from my face, to Bean in the sled, then back to me. His forehead creases in concern. He moves as if he's going to hug me, and I dodge away.

"Is Bean hurt?"

"Genius, he's in the sled. What do you think?"

"Oh man. That was crazy. They just ran off! Like, don't they come when they're called?"

"The dogs don't know 'stop.' They only know 'go.'" My voice is carefully neutral.

"I didn't . . . I told you . . . "

"Yeah, I know, you don't know how." My anger erupts like foam climbing up the neck of a soda bottle. I yell in his face, "You don't know how to do anything!"

Chris gives me an incredulous stare, then his face hardens. "I never said I knew anything about dogsledding! If you know everything, why weren't you driving the team?" He flings his arm, gesturing toward the dogs. "I'm so sick of your superior attitude. Why are you so angry all the time? And bossy! Don't you get tired of being mean?"

His words gut-punch me. "Maybe you're too busy dreaming about shopping malls to notice that we're *lost* out here thanks to *you!*"

"I told you, I'm sorry about the map, but this is not all my fault! You know, sometimes stuff just happens that you can't control."

"And I don't know how I'm going to feed the dogs. And now Bean is hurt!" My voice breaks, betraying me, and I turn my face away. In the sudden silence, my stomach gurgles. I find a water bottle and take a long swig.

Chris kicks at the snow. He rubs his face with his hands and, after a slight pause, says in a lower tone, "So you're yelling at me about being from the city, but what you're really mad at is that we don't have anything to eat, right? I'm worried about that too, you know. You might feel better if you tell me what you're really worried about instead of keeping it all to yourself."

He pauses again and looks at me hopefully. "Maybe we could fish for food. We keep seeing that river beside the trail, maybe there's fish in it. Dogs eat fish, don't they?"

I see in his face all of my own worry and fear mirrored back to me. He's trying hard to help. I know it's not all his fault.

"We don't have any fish hooks or line," I say.

"Hmm. Well, we'll think of something." He almost looks shy as he searches my face. "And there's lots I know how to do, Secret. Like, I'm a fast swimmer. I used to be on the swim team—won some medals, too."

"That's not very helpful at the moment." But I imagine being able to stay afloat, propel myself where I want to go, and I'm sort of envious.

"Right. Can't impress you. Well, I can't fix a sled, but I can fix your computer."

"Again, not very helpful. And I don't have a computer."

"You don't . . . what?"

"Well, my mom has one for work, but it doesn't have anything else on it. When would I have time to play on a computer? I told you, I'm a musher. I win races. My dogs and I win races."

"But . . . everyone has a computer!" He stares at me as if I've suddenly developed a unibrow.

"Well, I don't." I hold the water bottle up to him as a peace offering. "Anyway, we should keep going. I'm sure we'll see a road soon. Bean needs to get to a vet. And the longer we stay out here with no food, the more danger we're in of becoming hypothermic."

I don't mention the fact that now we're both wet from all the running and sweating. My inner clothes stick to my skin, a recipe for disaster out here that is so ingrained in me that I can't ignore the icy dread lodged in my gut.

Chris takes a sip of water and then points the bottle down the trail. "Our supper just went that way. Maybe if I whittle you a spear, you can throw that instead. I saw it in a movie once, I think."

I pretend I'm not listening to him as I pull off my anorak and shake out the snow.

"Or we could use this thing." Chris waves Mr. Minky toward me, then makes stabbing motions with it. "Dig a pit. Fill it with sharp sticks and the moose will fall in and impale himself. I know I've seen that in a movie. Except, it was a dude who fell, messed up his leg."

I glance at the dogs. They roll on the trail and snort. The fight is forgotten and they're all friends again. When I bend over Bean to check his wounds I see the puncture is still bleeding. Gently, I take the snow out of the gauze on his shoulder.

"Yikes, what happened to him?"

"I think he got kicked by the moose, or his leg's been pulled. He's got ligament or tendon damage. I don't know. But it's swelling so it needs to be iced in short sessions like this for a full day." I am not going to fail Bean.

"Stay here on the brake." I emphasize my words by making a show of holding the handlebar and standing solid on the brake. "Please."

Chris rolls his eyes at me and takes my place on the brake.

I walk back along the trail and collect myself. I look for my snowshoes and hat, not really expecting to see them. The snowshoes aren't that big a deal, but I need my hat.

I scan over the moose tracks and almost smile remembering my warrior woman move with the snowshoe. But then I think of Bean and my brow furrows. He needs a vet. And rest. He can't be allowed to run with that injury. And that means not having him in lead. I realize how much I've always depended on his intelligence. And now that we know there's a moose somewhere up ahead, we'll have to be extra careful.

When I hook the dogs back up, I put Drift up front with Blue and move Gazoo into wheel beside Dorset. Not every dog can lead. Some won't even run at all if they have dogs behind them. Too much pressure. Drift is my best option right now without Bean. I hop on beside Chris and call to the dogs.

"Ready? All right!"

We continue on, heading directly into the sun that's sinking fast behind the trees over the next ridge. My belly rumbles. A shiver runs down my back from the dampness of my sweat-soaked shirt. I glance down at Bean curled up in the bag. All our lives depend on what's ahead.

17

DUSK COMES WITH THE SAME SWIFTNESS as the previous night. I keep listening for sounds of traffic or snowmobiles—anything to give a hint of where we are. But there's nothing except the panting of dogs, the shushing of the runners sliding in the snow, and the light tinkling of the dogs' neckline clips.

Even as I wish for a road, my jaw tightens with

the knowledge we're going to have to spend another night out here. *What am I going to feed the dogs tonight?* What comes after that, I no longer allow myself to think about.

Perhaps we should've stayed back at our last camp. We could've tried to make a trap or fish hooks. I could maybe make a fish hook using the small forked branches on a tree. Maybe Chris's idea of a spear wasn't far off.

I shake my head. Then we wouldn't have found that wolf kill. We desperately needed those scraps of moose meat. But now, I don't think we'll be as lucky tonight.

I shiver again and adjust Dorset's dog coat around my head. It may look ridiculous, but without my hat, my ears and head were going to freeze. I had to improvise. The coat isn't really working, with a big open hole at the top, but at least it's blocking the wind from going down my neck. We're in serious trouble now. I can feel the onset of hypothermia like a snake slithering down my back.

I busy myself studying the dogs. Drift is an easily distracted leader, but thankfully Blue is keeping her straight. Everyone seems to be pulling, ears forward, tails straight, tuglines tight—except for Whistler. *Why is she limping?*

When I stop the team, they all dive into the snow. I leave the sled to Chris and walk down the line of dogs. Whistler snuffles in my ear as I bend over her. I inspect each foot separately, spreading apart the toes with my bare fingers. She has always had tender feet. Her fur seems to collect more snowballs than any of the other dogs'. I check her right front paw and see irritated red skin on the webbing between two toes.

Oh, no. With my fingers, I try to break apart the ice chunks stuck to her fur. The center ball is too tough to break, so I use my teeth. She licks my hand.

"Whistler, I'm sorry, girl."

"What's wrong?" Chris asks.

I trudge toward the sled and search for the bag of dog booties. "Whistler is getting a rub on her foot.

It's from this grainy snow. If I don't bootie her, she'll get a blister."

I tear through the gear in the sled, and Bean watches with interest. "Have you seen a blue bag full of fleece booties in here?"

"No."

I thought I had brought the bag. Did I bring the bag? I can't remember.

"You didn't dump it when you were looking for the tape?" I ask.

"I didn't dump anything. Would you give me a break?"

"Well, it's not in here. Great. What am I going to do without booties?" I hear my voice quaver and I take a breath. *Do not cry over missing booties.* The extra stress adds to my list of worries, and knots the narrow space between my eyes.

"Can you use like a mitt or something?"

Chris has been learning about dogsledding so fast, I forget how much he still doesn't know.

"No."

My shame at forgetting the booties tastes like bile in my mouth. "And besides, she'll need four booties. All her feet are going to look like this soon."

"Okay." Chris's reasonable tone irks me even more. "Well, we should be close to home now, right? We'll probably get there before she needs four booties."

I think Chris understands full well that we're probably *not* close to home. There is a big empty space of what we're not saying and it hangs over us like a vulture.

I sort through what's left in the first-aid kit and find Vaseline. Dipping a finger into the cold goo, I coat the fur between her toes to stop the snow from sticking. I think of the special Musher's Magic Foot Ointment that's also in the bootie bag. But I can't fix the fact that I didn't bring it, so I double-check her other paws to make sure they're free of ice balls then coat them with the Vaseline, too. My bare fingers quickly grow stiff with cold. I have to keep tucking them into my armpits.

The rest of the team lies on their bellies, shoveling mouthfuls of snow as they wait for me. Their mouths are covered in frost. I decide to check everyone's feet while I'm at it, even though there's nothing to be done if I do find more rubs. It puts my mind at ease to see everyone else has happy paws.

When that's done, I shove my frozen hands into my mitts, and head back to the sled to check on Bean. His shoulder is still tender and swollen.

"You take good care of them, Secret," Chris says quietly.

This small kindness is meant to make me feel better, I know, but it only makes my throat tighten. I lift my chin, call to the dogs, and we continue down the darkening trail.

As we go, I plan how we're going to find supper.

We should definitely make more tea. I could get Chris to build a fire while I set snares. Dad taught me to do that when I was eight. But what can I use? Laces from my mukluks? Who am I kidding? I need snare wire.

I stare at Bean while I think. *Poor Bean.* Is he getting thinner, too, or is it just my imagination? My concern about feeding the dogs is ripping a hole through me.

The more I think about food, the more my stomach tightens and cramps. That wolf-killed moose this morning seems like days ago. I rub at the headache between my eyebrows. It's dangerous to be working like this in the cold without food. Especially now that we're wet. And especially for some of us wearing cotton jeans.

We should stop here and build a fire to get dry again. But the tiny hope that we're close to finding a road makes me want to keep going while we still have some light. I peer around us and consider camping right here. Just the thought of trudging through deep snow without snowshoes to look for firewood exhausts me. I feel as weak as a newborn puppy.

"I'm pretty hungry," Chris says. "And I'm really cold."

"You talk a lot for someone who burns maps."

Chris looks at me sharply and I give him a slight hip check. He mock punches me in the arm, then grabs at the handlebar again as we bump over a ridge in the trail.

I watch Whistler and wonder if I should put her in the sled bag, too. It will seriously slow us down, but what else can I do? We need the dogs to get us out, so I have to take care of them. But we also need to make time. Our clock is running out. The problem spins 'round and 'round in my head.

I desperately wish I were a child again, riding in the sled, all wrapped up in blankets. Without any responsibilities or fears. Dad would lean over and peer down at me with gentle eyes. "You all snug, my little bug?" he'd ask. I could let Dad worry about everything. Just watch the dogs running, and enjoy the trees flashing past, and dream of the day I'd be old enough to run a junior musher race. Dad could worry about his trapline, and his guiding business, and making enough money to feed the dogs, and training the yearlings, and wondering why Blister had gone off her feed, and what to bring with us to stay warm and dry, and how to stay vigilant for when the wild woke up angry.

"You'll make such a good little musher, Icky. I'm so proud of you."

It seemed as if he'd always be there.

After the accident, it was impossible to believe he was gone. It wasn't real. Now, it seems the more I grasp at these memories, the more slippery they become.

Blue glances over his shoulder at me. I feel the dogs pick up and pull harder. Something must be on the trail. I peer into the shadows ahead. The moose has haunted us for these last few hours. Every dark trunk is a charging moose. The constant worry around each corner has my nerves swollen and exposed.

The dogs definitely sense something ahead. My pulse quickens. Blue looks back at me again and I stop the team.

"What is it, Blue?" My stomach drops. I grab the hatchet from the sled bag and hurry up the line to stand in front of him. What I'm going to do with a hatchet, I'm not sure. I keep trying to swallow down my fear as I peer down the trail. No sign of any moose, but she's still ahead somewhere.

"What now?" Chris asks.

"I don't know." My voice is high-pitched. I clear my throat. "Let them follow behind me." I keep plodding through the snow in front of the leaders with knees that feel like putty. My tense muscles spasm in the cold and I have to stop as a violent shiver goes through me.

We creep around a sharp bend grown in with dogwood and willow and I try to peer through the spaces between the trees. My mouth is dry. I wipe at the base of my nose.

I see nothing ahead but more snow. Darkness cloaks the trail as the sky bleeds into the trees. My arm is almost numb from the death grip I have on the hatchet and I try to relax my fingers. I switch hands and swing my arm in circles. I'm just about to turn back when a glint in the trees makes me snap my head around.

"It's a cabin!" I press a hand over my chest as the tension drains from my body.

18

I FEEL SO GOOD, I ACTUALLY CLAP my hands and hop in place like some moronic cheerleader. But with a hatchet, instead of pompoms.

"It's a trapper's cabin!" I turn and hug Blue. He knew it. He had tried to tell me about it.

"Woo hoo! Think there's food?"

"I hope so! Come on, let's go check." I don't see

a trail from where we are so I plunge off the path, eager to make my own. And sink to my waist in soft powder. "But not this way."

I climb back to where the dogs are watching me with amusement. Blue's tongue hangs in a silent laugh. I motion for Chris to let the dogs go and I grab the sled as it slides by. Chris beams at me from his runner and then grabs me with one arm and awkwardly crushes me into his side. I grin right back with abandon, feeling absolutely giddy with joy. Our eyes connect with the shared delight of the moment.

"But do we still get to sleep in the sled bag?" he asks.

"You can if you really want to. I'll be inside in a bed." My smile feels as if it's cracking my frozen face in half. We found a trapper's cabin. We're on the right trail.

When we pull up to the front porch, I'm disappointed there aren't any fresh tracks. No snowmobiles or movement. But there are signs of use. A gas can sits under the layer of snow on the front step. Cut and split wood is stacked under an open-air shed. There's an indent in the snow from the cabin to the outhouse where a trampled trail lies under the fresh snow and another one that heads behind the cabin. The cabin is in good shape, too. Curtains cover the windows and a pair of willow-twig chairs sit in a corner by the front door.

I tromp up the steps and check the door, which is locked.

"What the heck is this?" Chris points to strips of wood under each window that have nails facing pointed-side out like porcupines along the length.

"Bear proofing," I say. "That's a big furry animal with long claws that likes to break into camps when no one is home."

"Okay, okay. City folks actually know what bears are. We've seen them in Coke commercials." Chris cups his hands to his face and presses it against the window where the curtains separate. "Are we gonna break in?"

"Give me a second." I follow the trail to the out-house and peer into a coffee can with a lid. Inside is a roll of toilet paper, and a key. I don't know this trap-per, but I know about trap cabins. Ours was passed down from Grandpa to Dad. Then to another trapper shortly after Dad died. I've never been back there.

I reappear from the outhouse and triumphantly hold up the key. Chris whistles appreciatively.

"My dad was a trapper," I say.

"Was?"

"Um, yeah." I pause. "He died over a year ago."

Chris raises his eyebrows.

"He was out alone last January, without me or the dogs. He fell through the ice and got swept down-stream. He drowned."

Chris watches me for a beat, and then nods in silence.

"Ah," he says simply.

I take a moment to breathe. This is the most I've

ever said about Dad's death. Everyone already knew what happened; I didn't have to explain. And I didn't talk about it with anyone. Not with Sarah, not Uncle Leonard, especially not with my mom— no one. Now that it's done, I realize telling Chris wasn't that hard.

"I'll settle the dogs." I hand the key to Chris, nodding toward the cabin, then turn to the team.

Bean is still in the sled, asleep on top of the gear, but lifts his head when I approach. His tail thumps on the sleeping bag. I struggle to pick him up, but I'm so weak that it brings on the shakes in my legs and my breathing becomes wheezy. He limps heavily toward the front of the team and I have to fight back tears. With that injury, he shouldn't be moving around at all.

I wonder if he'll accept coming into the cabin where it's warmer. Though it might be too warm for him, and stress him even more. The dogs would rather be outside where they are acclimated. I agonize over what to do as I stake out the rest of the dogs along the drop line. They are unusually quiet — so tired and hungry.

My eyes strain in the darkness of the woodshed until I find what I had hoped. I let out a huge breath. Bales of straw are stacked along the far wall. Maybe the trapper has a husky, too. Smiling, I lay out bedding along the drop line as the dogs frisk and roll in it with glee. Dorset collects a big pile with her paws like a gambler raking in chips and rolls her neck over it.

Bean groans as he flops onto the pile I placed beside him. I pack fresh snow under the gauze still wrapping his shoulder and inspect the puncture wound. It's finally stopped bleeding. I notice with alarm that my hands are shaking. I need to get out of these wet clothes and get warm *now*.

The fading light is making way to a dark purple and black skyline as I trudge up the cabin steps. We found this place just in time. When I step inside, Chris is hanging a lamp on a hook from the ceiling. It throws shadows on the walls and lights the dim interior.

"Took me a while to figure out how to light this thing," he says with obvious pride. "Pretty sweet digs, huh?"

There are bunk beds on the far wall, a pot-bellied wood stove, and a kitchen with a sink and curtains covering cupboards underneath. A small table in the center with two chairs is the only other furniture.

Chris heads to the kitchen and starts rummaging. I open the stove and toss in a handful of kindling from the wood box beside it. I stuff birch bark underneath and light it. The loud snaps and pops fill the small room. Immediately, I stick my hands, palms up, in front of the little flames.

"What have we here?" Chris holds aside the curtain to show me a shelf full of metal tins. He opens one and his eyes light up as if he's just won the lottery.

"Cookies!" He stuffs two into his mouth and

crunches. "Mmm." His grin is contagious and I'm walking over to take one when I spot a wooden box on the floor.

"Oh, that looks promising," I say. Peering inside, I let out a little cry. "Snare wire!"

Chris eyes me as I pull the spool of wire and a pair of snips out of the box. "You can catch something with that? Looks like wire to make jewelry."

I nod. Our luck has finally improved. Now we have means for feeding ourselves. "This is for—oh!" I spot a dish on the floor. "He does have a dog." My gaze darts around the room, searching. And then I spot a large metal garbage can in the corner. When I race over and lift the lid, my heart skips a beat.

"Dog food!"

The can is full to the top with kibble.

19

ANOTHER SHIVER TAKES HOLD AND I realize I have
to get warm before I do anything else. I can't care for
my dogs if I'm too cold and weak.

"We have to take our wet clothes off," I say.

Chris looks amused with his cheeks full of cookie. "Oo tryin' to het ee naked?" With the *k* in the
last word, crumbs fly out of his mouth.

"Oh, that's charming. No, you definitely keep yours on. I'll time you to see how long before hypothermia sets in." I grab a plastic bag from the bunks, and dump out two wool blankets. Chris is clearly even more impressed with this find.

"I call bottom bunk," he says.

I turn my back to show him I want some privacy, and start peeling off wet clothes. I stop when I'm down to my underwear and thin polypro undershirt. Then I wrap myself in a scratchy wool blanket that smells musty but is dry and warm.

"Okay," I say to Chris, and turn around.

He's also wrapped in a blanket and when he turns, he pulls two chairs toward the wood stove with one hand while awkwardly holding his blanket closed with the other. We sit together in front of the fire, eating cookies. I stuff one in my mouth, then busy myself making snares to avoid looking at Chris's bare shoulders sticking out of his blanket.

The fire crackles, giving off delicious heat. Snipping off a section of the wire, I feel a strange need to continue our conversation from before. "I usually went with him every weekend."

Chris doesn't ask who I'm talking about, just nods, and continues crunching his cookies. He shifts slightly forward, bringing his knee so close to mine, I feel its warmth.

"And the dogs pretty much always went with him. But they'd been working hard on the trapline, and I'd run them in a big race the weekend before. Dad wanted to give them some time off. And he was going to the farthest line in his area; he said the old snowmobile would be best."

I snip off another piece of wire, my fingers working automatically. Make a loop at the end, pull the other end of the wire through, crook it slightly to hold the snare open.

"Mom wanted me to go to Fairbanks with her that day to help shop for my nana. I told her Dad needed my help with the line. She said for me to stop being so dramatic. That he'd been out before with-out me, that he didn't need to always have me or the dogs with him. She made me stay with her . . . " I'm about to explain that if I'd been there with him as I should've been, I could've saved him. But as I say the words aloud, I hesitate for the first time, searching for the truth.

I shake my head. "I was so mad. I hated her for not understanding what it's like to run dogs. What it's like in the bush. You have to trust your dogs. Dad always told me that. We worked together, you know?"

I drop another snare at my feet and reach for the spool again. It feels good telling all this to some-one, to say it out loud. I'd never even been able to talk about it with Sarah because she already knew the story. Talking to Chris was easier because he doesn't know anyone.

"Anyway, that's why I'm afraid of water, since the accident. Actually, I was afraid before the accident. I never liked swimming in the lake— there's pike down there." I grimace.

Chris gives a short laugh that startles me. I'm so used to people feeling sorry for me after they find out.

"You're afraid of pike? Like, the fish?" He sticks his lips out pretending to blow bubbles and waves his hands behind his ears like gills.

It makes me laugh. "They grow big here, you know." I swipe at his arm with my snippers. "And they have enormous teeth! I've heard stories of somebody's Chihuahua falling off a dock and getting picked off by a giant pike!"

"I can't picture you being afraid of anything." He shakes his head. "And swimming is easy! I can teach you." He seems completely pleased with learning this about me.

"Yeah, I think I'll pass on that. Anyway, my clothes are dry enough now. I should go check on the dogs, and get some water." I suddenly can't wait to get the dog food soaking.

Out of habit, I reach for my compass that's usually around my neck and frown. It's gone. I immediately miss its comforting shape and weight, and get a shiver of fear. It must've been lost during my drag behind the team. I try to shrug it off. It's not as if I've used it much since we lost the map. But the sense of security it gave me is gone, as if my compass didn't just help me find the direction to take but helped steer me in life as well.

Leaving Chris in charge of the fire, I quickly pull on my thermal long underwear that's still damp, but my base layer is dry next to my skin. The door squeaks as I step onto the porch. I stop, blinking in the dim light. The sun has long set, and I can see only as far as the light stretching out from the cabin windows.

Once my eyes adjust, I take my time visiting with each of the dogs. Dorset is still celebrating the straw. Her eyes dance, which makes my eyes dance. Even my worry about Bean fades with the happiness I feel knowing they'll get dinner tonight.

I unload the sled and pile the gear on the front steps. Then I find an empty metal bucket in the woodshed and fill it with snow. My muscles protest when I try to carry more than two pieces of wood.

When I wonder what we would have done if we hadn't found this cabin, I envision a somber scene with the two of us too weak to get out of the sled. Of the dogs wondering why we aren't feeding them. Perhaps the wolves coming for our bodies. Then for the dogs . . . I shiver, and try to shake the image out of my head. We've found the cabin. We're safe.

Chris feels safer to me now, too. Talking with someone who doesn't see me as a wounded child is a relief. Mom is wounded, too. And maybe it's not all her fault. I shake my head and start back to the cabin, too tired to think of this now.

20

INSIDE, THE WOOD STOVE IS CHEERFULLY crackling. I set the bucket on the stove and it hisses and steams.

"Already found some water," Chris says, pointing to two large plastic pails. He's hanging the dog harnesses and his jeans on a rope he's rigged up, and is wearing a threadbare plaid shirt and a pair of wool pants with suspenders. The pants bag out around him like a circus clown's.

I find myself admiring the way the shirt stretches between his shoulder blades. His swimming shoulders, I guess. The shirt's long sleeves are loosely rolled, and the collar just touches the curls at the back of his neck.

Chris turns suddenly from the clothesline, and I drop my gaze to the pails. When I peer inside, I see they're both full of icy water. Chris hovers over the buckets, acting as if he birthed them himself.

"The trail behind the cabin leads to a creek," he says, beaming. "And look what else I found." He pulls a small envelope from his pocket. I'm unsure what it is so I shake my head.

"It's a sewing kit! We can make Whistler some booties."

"Oh! That's a great idea!" I wonder if there's some spare fleece around here. Then I remember my complete ineptitude in my previous attempts at sewing, creating hideously misshapen things that would probably make the problem with her feet even worse.

I thoroughly wish that I'd learned to sew. It's not as if my mom didn't try to teach me, but I am obviously missing the gene that allows for it. I seriously can't even sew on a button.

Chris looks at me in confusion.

"I'm a little rusty with the sewing skills."

Chris stuffs the kit back into his pocket. "Who's talking about you?"

"You can sew? Why do you know how to sew?"

"I like making things, okay?"

I shrug and then notice the table. It's neatly set with bowls, spoons, and mugs. A lit candle sits in the center.

I raise my eyebrows and Chris bows dramatically, his eyes lit with a glint of mischief.

"The dogs get fed first," I say, though my stomach twists painfully when I think of food. I pour slushy water into the metal bucket with the snow. Then I scoop kibble into it up to the brim. I set it back on the stove. "They're having a warm dinner."

"Well, Secret, I think we both deserve a warm dinner, too." He dips a pot into the water and sets it beside the bucket on the stove. Then he opens an envelope of soup mix and dumps it into the pot. "Fending off moose is hungry work."

"I don't remember you doing anything but screaming." I laugh at his mock look of surprise. Then I laugh harder at his reenactment of my snowshoe fling. He pretends he's the moose and grabs his nose, wobbles around the table.

"Okay, Mr. Moose. I need your help to set these snares while we wait for supper to cook."

He stands straight. "Me? I'm not much of a trapper."

"That's okay. You can hold the light." I point to the lantern. "We need to set these tonight if we hope to eat breakfast in the morning." I grab the six prepared snares and the hatchet from the sled.

We head toward the river, where I saw a small stand of willow and stunted spruce trees. Chris tramps behind me in the same deep footprints that I'm making. I hold the lantern out in front of me as I scan the snow ahead.

"There!" I point to a worn trail through the trees. "That's a snowshoe hare run. They've been coming through here. The tracks are fresh."

We follow the trail till we get to what looks like the narrowest spot between the brush. I stop, and Chris crashes into me.

"Would you pay attention? You're worse than the dogs."

Chris huffs in my ear. "What are you doing now?"

I hand him the lantern and reach to hack at an alder sapling. "I'm going to tie the snare to this pole, wedge it into the snow so the wire hangs over the trail, right where they run through, see?" I adjust the alder so the wire hangs about three inches off the ground, like Dad had shown me.

"So, we get to eat meat tomorrow?" Chris shines the light directly in my eyes as he turns to me.

"That's the idea," I say, holding my hand out to block the light.

I complete the set by breaking off a few twigs and placing them strategically next to the snare to hold it open, and keep it hidden. Then I rise, brushing snow off my knees. "See? Easy. Now you can do the next one."

I'm strangely proud as I coach Chris over the next few sets. I'm also annoyed when he falls into one and snares his own foot, ruining that run with his tracks, but when it comes to Chris, I'm getting used to it. We stomp back to the cabin, joking and shoving each other. It feels so good to have some control over this situation. We can set snares to feed ourselves. This changes everything. Maybe we can survive out here.

The dogs' dinner is soaked. As I carry the bucket down the stairs, Blue is the first to sound the alarm. All six leap to their feet, barking hysterically.

Chris hangs the lantern on the woodshed, then holds the two dishes out as I plop some of the contents from the bucket. He puts the dishes in front of the first two dogs, Bean and Drift. They pounce, making slurping noises as they gulp the food. I smile wide. My dogs are eating.

I feed the rest of the dogs down the line as Chris visits with Blue.

"Look at his eyes!" He tentatively pets the dog's head.

Predictably, Blue jams his nose under Chris's legs. "Whoa!" The dog buries his head then lifts his muzzle up as he's done with me a hundred times.

"He wants you to scratch his back." I don't mention that Chris has come a long way from being terrified of the dogs.

On the other side of me, Dorset lies on her back on her nest with her back legs spread indecently. Chris laughs and rubs her belly.

After Bean has finished his bowl, I remove the

snow pack from his shoulder and take the wet gauze off. His gash is weeping clear fluid, and I bite my lip. I can't imagine a worse scenario than having a dog with an infection out here and not having anything to give him for it. I consider carrying him to the cabin, but almost as if he senses what I'm thinking, he drops down again to his bed of straw. He stares up at me as if to say he's staying put. I pat his head and nod. "Okay, chum. Whatever makes you happy."

"He's going to be okay, right?" Chris asks, kneeling down to smooth the fur sticking up around Bean's ruff.

"Maybe, if he gets to rest that shoulder. But he still needs a vet."

Bean closes his eyes under Chris's light touch. The sight makes my chest tighten, and I fight to push down the fear for my lead dog. I have to get him to a vet for antibiotics and anti-inflammatory drugs.

"Let's go eat," I say. "I'm starving."

21

WE LEAVE THE DOGS TO SLEEP off their full bellies. I send a silent prayer to Dad to heal Bean overnight. When we enter the cabin again, the wall of heat hits me. That combined with the smell of chicken noodle soup, and I almost fall over.

"Wow, we're going to be warm tonight!" I shed my outer clothes, and hang them to finish drying along with the dog coats and harnesses. Steam already leaks from the harnesses, giving off a bouquet of wet dog.

"So what does a dog bootie look like?" Chris asks, tightening his clothesline.

"It's like a little fleece sock that fits over their foot. Not too big that it would bunch up on them, but wide enough that lets their toes splay out when they run. They stay on by attaching a piece of Velcro on the top to cinch on their leg." I use my hand to show Chris what I mean, not really believing he'll be able to make anything that Whistler can use. Then I pour soup into both bowls on the table.

"I hope the owner doesn't mind us borrowing all this stuff." Chris sits, pulling up his oversized pants.

I ignore the spoon and grab the warm bowl with both hands. Just holding the bowl is heaven. I slurp loudly, and actually feel the soup travel the whole journey down.

"Its bush law," I say around a mouthful of noodles. "If anyone's in trouble out here, you use what you need, then replace it later." The hot golden liquid gushes sensually around in my empty belly.

Chris puts down his spoon and copies me with his own bowl.

"Aaah," he says with feeling, then gulps another mouthful before putting the bowl down and waving his hand over it to cool it.

"What we really need is a snowmobile. Too bad he didn't leave one of those laying around."

"I think that's the last thing you need. Where did you learn to drive anyway?"

"Well, I've never actually been on one before."

"Shocking." I gulp another mouthful and close my eyes briefly. "So no snowmobiling in Toronto, and not much snow. Sounds pretty boring."

"It's not! And I didn't spend all my time at the mall, as you seem to think."

I drop four cubes of sugar into my mug with a tea bag. The coffee creamer packets look a little suspicious with some sort of mold growing on their corners, so I pass on those. I reach for the kettle on the stove that Chris had filled as well, and pour the hot water into my mug.

"That's good because you'd be disappointed with our sad excuse for a mall. It's really just a row of stores. There's Wicker's feed store, the grocery store, the post office and trading post, the coffee shop, and the pool hall. The pool hall actually burned down. Twice. But half the kids in my class hang there anyway."

"Not you?"

"No. I . . . I don't really have time to hang out."

"Huh. Shocking," Chris repeats, and then slurps more soup. He reaches for the tin of crackers, and adds half its contents to his bowl, creating a mound of crumbs escaping back onto the table. He gives me a big satisfied smile as he pats his stomach.

"So where *did* you spend all your time?" I grab a handful of crackers and stuff them into my mouth. The crunch and salt of them fills me with reverence for Mr. Saltine.

"I just hung out, you know, over at the Trap and Skeet club. It's next to the snare wire depot."

"Do you even know what 'skeet' means?"

Chris laughs. "Okay. I told you, I swim. Competitively. I used to practically live at the pool. Practiced twice a day prepping for the big meets."

"So, you're good?"

"I'm better than good. My relay team wasn't too happy with me moving. No one can touch my fly."

I laugh. "Humble much?"

"I'm just saying." Chris puffs out his chest. "So you're going to have the best teacher when we start your lessons. I cannot wait to start showing you something that I can do, finally."

"Yeah, that's not happening."

"What? Why? You're afraid of what might happen when you see me in a Speedo, aren't you?"

I curl my lip at him. "Gross! I'll be running the other way is what will happen." Feeling my neck heat up, I down my soup and rise in one quick motion so Chris doesn't have the satisfaction of watching me blush.

I bring my empty dish to the sink, gulping the rest of my tea, and gag on something. When I check the bottom of my mug I see what looks like a clump of hair.

"What the . . . "

"What?" Chris asks.

I stride back to the kettle on the stove and open the lid. I slosh the water around and peer into the dark depths. There's something in there. When I dump the contents into the sink, my stomach heaves.

Lying in the sink is a very dead, bald mouse.

I clutch my belly and whirl around. "Didn't you check the kettle before you filled it?"

"Uh, check it for what?" Chris peers into his own half-finished tea.

I shrug, looking pointedly at the sink. Watching his face as he figures it out is almost worth the imagined grit in the back of my throat.

22

WEDNESDAY

AFTER A DEEP, DREAMLESS SLEEP ON the top bunk, I wake sore from yesterday's drag behind the dogs. Hard to believe that was only yesterday. Stretching into a sitting position, I find gifts at the end of my bed.

Four little dog booties lay in a row next to a wool hat that has even been lined with what I recognize as the curtain off the kitchen shelves. The booties have been made from what looks like another pair of wool pants, wherever Chris found them.

A piece of tape from the first-aid kit should work to keep them on Whistler's feet. I pull them inside out and inspect the seams, widening my eyes in amazement. Tiny, even stitches run up the length of the booties as if they'd been professionally sewn. The hat could be store bought, it's so well shaped. I snug it on to find it fits perfectly.

How does Chris know how to sew? Picturing him bent over a sewing machine at home makes me shake my head. The more I learn about him, the more I realize how much I don't know.

How long have we been out here? What feels like months has hardly been a week. I count backwards . . . two, three nights. We've been out here four days. I know Mom will not have slept this whole time. It will seem like months for her, too.

I lean over the side of the bunk to peek down at Chris, and all I see is his hair sticking up in all directions. He's burrowed under a wool blanket that has four bootie-shaped holes cut out of it along with a chunk missing from the side.

"Hey! Milquetoast. Stove duty." I jump off the bunk and head for my outer clothes. I feel so much stronger today. Amazing what a warm night's rest can do. Now we need some protein. I can't wait to check our trapline.

But Bean comes first.

The fire has long since died so the cabin floor creaks in the cold. I adjust my new hat and smile. Once again, it's as if Bean can sense me, because a howl starts up outside.

"Pitter-patter, let's get at 'er." Dad's words come out of my mouth.

The long hump on the bottom bunk stirs as I head out the door. The dog song ends abruptly as the door shuts behind me. Six pairs of eyes swivel toward me expectantly.

"Breakfast soon, guys. Just me for now."

I crunch toward the drop line and right away notice something under Dorset's curled-up body. When I get closer, I see it's a blanket on top of her straw. Dorset lies in the center of it and thumps her tail at my approach.

"Looks like you've got yourself a friend, Dorset. When did he give this to you?"

Chris would have had to come out here after I fell asleep. By himself. And the dogs are so used to him, they didn't make a sound.

I kneel in the snow beside Bean. He's standing, his face coated in gray frost. He's not putting any weight on his leg, but his eyes shine. I suddenly have a lump in my throat and hug him fiercely to me.

My dogs. What was I thinking trying to get better leaders? I have the best dogs in the world.

"What do you think of this computer geek, Bean? Do you think he's strange?" I gently run my fingers along his shoulder, feeling for any improvement. "I think you like him, but you don't want to admit it."

The swelling might be down a little, but it's where the swelling is that scares me. It's a serious injury, definitely a tear. "You won't be running anywhere for a while, Beanie. Don't want to wreck that leg for life."

The puncture looks normal, it will heal fine, but the gash is meaty and deep with an angry redness. I frown at it, wishing again for antibiotics. Bean noses my hand and I force a smile, trying to look unconcerned.

A jarring, ear-splitting explosion shatters my thoughts. All the dogs jump. Dorset lets out a startled yip. I leap to my feet, confused for a moment, staring at the cabin.

"What the . . ." *Chris! Oh, no!*

Finally, I react and sprint through the snow. My foot hits an icy patch and I spin out, falling hard. I jump back up and keep running. Blood pounds in my ears.

Horrific images play out in my mind. It sounded almost like a gunshot. Did he shoot himself? Is he dead? I didn't notice a gun in the cabin. Did someone else come and shoot him?

No, a gun wouldn't sound like that. A strangled noise chokes out of me as I reach the stairs, vault up two at a time, stumble to the door. I fling it open.

Chris is picking himself up from the floor. Smoke fills the room. The front door of the stove is missing, but then I see it by the bunks. A can of white gas for the lamp sits on the table and I glance back to the stove.

"Whoa . . . " Chris blinks at me.

He smells like burnt pig. His eyebrows are singed half off. A large burn hole covers the front of his jacket, but his shirt underneath looks untouched.

"I—I tried to light the fire." Chris looks around with a blank stare then sinks into the chair.

"With what?" My voice sounds shrill but I don't care. I glance at the can on the table.

"It was really cold in here," Chris says defensively. "I thought I'd light the fire quicker." He inspects the front of his jacket and lets out a groan.

"You didn't use *this,* did you?" I stride to the table and grab the fuel. When I pick it up, I punch it out toward him. I feel like I have a tsunami bubbling up inside me. "White gas is highly volatile."

"Well, now you tell me."

The tsunami rises to the surface, it rolls over me, and I burst out in hysterical laughter. Chris looks at me, shocked.

I laugh so hard that I double over and hold myself. "I leave you alone for two minutes," I gasp.

I'm scaring myself, my emotions are so uncontrollable. Why am I laughing? But I can't seem to stop. I suck in a breath and convulse in another fit of laughing.

Chris stands, looking panicked.

"How have you . . . gotten this far without killing yourself?" Tears roll down my face. I take a ragged breath. "You could've *died!*"

Suddenly, I let out a sob. More tears burst out and course down my cheeks. Everything that's happened seems to flood my mind at once. I literally feel like I will explode if anything else goes wrong.

I sob like I'm six years old. "I don't know where we are. I don't know how to get us home. I don't know why my Dad had to die!"

My chest heaves and I gulp down a racking breath. A mortifying hiccup escapes. My last words seem to echo and hang in the silence around us.

Chris stares at me with his singed eyebrows.

"Please don't use white gas again," I finally say.

"Trust me, I won't," Chris says softly, and then adds, "I'm really sorry your dad died, Vicky."

It's the first time he's said my name and somehow it helps. I breathe deeply. "Me too."

23

I WIPE AT MY NOSE AS CHRIS picks up the stove door with a loud scrape across the floor. The smoke has thinned out in the room now.

"Some people use gas to start a fire quicker," he says. "I've seen it done — well, on TV."

"They don't use white gas, I can tell you that."

"I just wanted to help." Chris fits the door back

on the hinges. It squeals as he tries to swing it closed. "I didn't know it would blow up like that." He feels his eyebrows.

I'm not used to seeing Chris without his grin. He props a piece of kindling against the stove door to keep it shut, then nods as if he's fixed it. He backs up to the table and sinks in a chair, taking a drink of water. When he wipes his mouth with the back of his hand, he sucks in a breath and looks at it. "I burned my hands."

"You're lucky you didn't burn the whole camp down. We should leave before you break anything else."

"Oh! You don't want to stay here in case someone comes? I sort of thought we'd stay."

Chris looks so dejected slumped in the chair with his singed hair and a red burn on his upper cheek. His forehead swelling has gone down, but the bruise and cut still remain.

I suddenly feel the need to cheer him up. I

realize I've been making all the decisions, and look where that has got us.

"We need to decide what to do. Together."

Chris stares at the wood stove, lost in thought. "Yeah, well one thing."

"What?"

"You tell me everything from now on. *Everything.* Okay?"

I nod and sit at the table across from him. "Okay. So I'm thinking that waiting for someone to rescue us doesn't sit well with me. There's no way of knowing how long we'd be waiting. This trapper may have filled his quota and be done for the season. He might not even be planning on coming back."

Chris sits up straighter.

"We've already eaten the food that's here. The dogs are fed now. We're dry and fed. We can bring that tin of cookies and the rest of the dog food with us. And now we have the snares, we can set them wherever we go. That reminds me, I haven't even checked them yet."

"How much farther do you think?"

"We can't be far now. We found this cabin." I sincerely hope we aren't far. I frown, and then remember that Chris just said that I should tell him everything I'm thinking. "But we also might get lost. So it's a gamble."

"We *are* lost." His shoulders sag again. "This completely sucks, eh?"

"You just said 'eh.'"

He blinks at me for a moment, then gives me a small grin. I smile back.

"How 'bout we travel west for half the day," I suggest, "and if we don't find a road, we'll turn around and come back here? Whistler hasn't even had a chance to try out her cool new booties."

Chris raises his eyes to mine.

"Deal," he says.

"And one more thing."

"Yeah?"

"It was me."

"Huh?"

I try to look contrite. "I'm the one who took off your mom's side mirror. As long as I'm telling you *everything*."

He grins wider. "Now I really want to get back. Gotta make sure you pay it off."

"Pay it off, how, exactly?"

"Oh, I don't know. Tokens, favors, an eternity of servitude— I'll think of something."

I'm so relieved to see his fire back, I don't even mind the teasing.

"One's better than nothing," I say to myself, hanging the hare behind my back as I gather the snares. When I walk past the dogs I proudly hold it out by its feet. The dogs watch me, and I could swear they nod with approval.

When I stomp back into the cabin, I feel as if I'm in one of Dad's old trapper movies, but *I'm* bringing home our next meal and Chris is cleaning the kitchen.

"Well, aren't you looking pleased with yourself?"

I hold up the hare and Chris's eyes grow round. "Wow! I didn't think rabbits would be so big!"

"This isn't a rabbit, it's a hare." I drop the snares on the table. "We can have half right now, and save the other half for lunch. We can cook it on the stove. We'll just leave the door open — it'll still work." My mouth waters thinking about a bubbling pot of meat. "Here, hold the feet."

Chris hesitantly reaches out. "Look at the size of these feet! They're as long as my hand!"

"Must be why they're called snowshoe hares. Hold tight." I grip the skin on the legs, just below where Chris is holding, and yank down forcefully. The skin rips at the ankles and turns neatly inside out down to the head, exposing the red meat.

"Wha — Holy naked hare!"

I set to work cutting off the back straps of meat while Chris makes a fire. I'm eager to get on the trail, but eating is number one. When we sink our teeth into breakfast, I could die from the sweet flavor. It doesn't take us long to finish the tiny pot. I consider cooking the second half right away, but decide we should save it, not knowing if we'll get lucky again.

We pack the rest of the hare with the last of the crackers along with our small pile of gear. The energy from breakfast courses through my body and makes me feel as if everything will be all right. We can do this. Yes, we're going home today.

24

THE DOGS ARE RARING TO GO as we hook up again. Chris is now able to harness Drift as she frantically digs, bawls, jumps, and spews white foam across his sleeve. The sled is loaded with extra supplies from the cabin, and Bean is perched on top of it all in the bag, his eyes telling me exactly how he feels about it. He impales me with the most forlorn stare. "I'm sorry, Bean, but I can't let you run." Whistler prances in her new booties. I take a final look around, pull the snow hook, and we charge out of the yard.

But the initial charge doesn't last long. The dogs slow their pace and I can see that they are in desperate need of a few days' rest.

"Homeward bound," Chris sings beside me on the runner. We've adopted a system of how to share the handlebar so we don't shove each other off balance. And the handlebar is indeed holding up well.

I tell Chris about each dog on the line as we travel. How I stayed awake all night when Bean's litter was born. I was ten years old. It was minus thirty outside so Dad had Bean's mom set up in the cloakroom. I watched the whole thing and saw Bean, Dorset, and Gazoo slide out, each in a glistening sac of goo, their little blind faces searching for a teat. They had looked like hamsters after a few days. Fat and furry. But it wasn't till they were four weeks old that they were fun to play with.

"How did Bean become a leader?"

We're climbing a hill and both of us jump off to run beside the sled and help the dogs pull it up.

"Good girl, Drift," I call.

"Look at her pull!" Chris says.

We crest the hill, and Chris and I jump on our runners again. I glance over and see his cheeks are red with the cold air. He beams at me as he huffs.

Whenever I would talk about running the dogs back home, Sarah's eyes would glaze over but I can see that Chris gets it. I turn back to the dogs. Everyone's pulling with tight tugs, just much slower than our normal racing pace. If the constant worry over Bean and the fear of being lost weren't pounding in my chest at all times, I'd actually be happy. How long had it been since I felt that?

"Bean just wanted to lead. You could tell. He

listened for my voice all the time in the team, and he kept trying to look ahead of the other dogs in front of him. Bean and I have had a special connection right from the start. He didn't even lead well for my dad."

My heart feels full as I look down at Bean. I see Chris's respect for him in the nod of his head.

"Dad had his own leader—Beetle. She's so bossy. She snaps at any dog beside her who isn't doing a good job. She's a great leader, but too grouchy for me."

"Uh-huh." Chris glances at me. "Sounds like someone . . . "

I decide to ignore that. "Bean is just there when you need him. So dependable. You should see him in a race. He's crazy-smart."

"Maybe I could go to your next race and watch," Chris says. Then he quickly adds, "See Bean in action. I'll park really far away."

I don't know what to say to that, so I just nod. But imagining crossing the finish line at my next race and having Chris there cheering makes me feel good.

An image of my mom comes to mind. Since Dad died, she doesn't come to my races. I haven't wanted her there. But today thinking of her at my next one feels good, too.

Ahead of us, the trail forks into two possible directions. "What do you think?" I ask.

"It doesn't look like one is more used than the other, does it?"

I check the position of the sun over my shoulder. "I think we should take the left and hope it keeps going west."

When the leaders arrive at the fork, I yell, "Haw, Blue."

He hesitates, glances at me, then heads left, dragging Drift with him. They trot over the snow, which has hardened and is easier going.

Chris pedals with his outside leg to help the sled forward. "We could go down here for another hour and then it'd be time to turn around."

We follow the trail out of the trees and into a

wide-open space. The bank of the river is visible on the far shore. The dogs keep following the packed surface and we slide down onto the edge of the ice. I stop the team.

"Whoa. Whoa." The dogs glance at me, questioning. Then face forward and bark.

"What's wrong?" Chris asks.

"It's a river."

"Well, if there's a trail crossing, it must be a solid river, no?"

I notice a half-buried wooden sign. Snow clings to its face so I can't read what it says, but my pulse quickens.

I stomp on the snow hook, then tromp through the deep snow to get closer to the sign. It's cracked and weathered and very old, but its presence here is significant. When I brush off the snow, I can barely see a hand-painted, faded arrow pointing up.

I turn to Chris with excitement. "It's a trail marker. There's something across the river!"

"Yes!"

I turn and study where the trail crosses the ice. I'd better check.

I wallow back onto the trail and stomp the snow off. "Don't worry, Bean. We're almost there. We're going to get you to a vet today." I give him a pat, then dig down into the sled bag and find the hatchet.

My pulse hammers in my ears as I walk out onto the ice.

I chop once. Twice. It looks good. I move forward. Chop a few more times. Still looks good. I move ahead again.

The dogs whine to follow, but Chris holds them by standing on the snow hook that digs into the packed snow on the trail.

I creep out using this method of testing that Dad had shown me.

"Always test a river," he said. "The current underneath can change the ice thickness from one spot to another. Take a few good chops with the blade. If

225

it doesn't go through, it's thick enough to hold your weight."

An unwelcome thought occurs: if this method works, then how did Dad fall through?

I'm halfway across, hands shaking, when I bend down to swipe at the thin snow cover to get a better look. The ice is a dark, opaque color and I can see cracks in the surface that look at least four inches thick. Plenty of ice.

I turn and hustle back to the team. "Looks safe. We'll just zip across on the trail here."

"That's what I was saying."

"Ready? All right!" The dogs surge forward and we slide onto the frozen river.

We're good. We're good. We're good, I chant to myself.

We're near the middle of the river, where the snow cover is thinnest, when I catch movement out of the corner of my eye. I glance downstream and suck in my breath.

Two otters are playing on the ice.

No.

Too late, Drift has seen them.

"NO!" I scream as she wheels around, dragging Blue with her. Then he sees them and, without Bean up there, I know I've lost.

I smash the metal points of the brake into the ice, but it doesn't do much good. On thin snow cover like this, I don't have any control if the dogs take off.

And the dogs take off.

We're flying down the middle of the river toward the otters. The dogs have suddenly found reserves of energy. The otters hear my screaming and look up, see the team bearing down on them, and turn to run. They have short little legs, but they can move fast when they want to. They hump along in front of us, just out of reach of the leaders.

"Blue, NO! Whoa!" I'm standing with all my weight on the brake. Chris has one foot on too, but we're still sliding forward. Rocks and stumps sticking out of the ice blur past.

No, no, no.

"Stand on the brake!" I scream at Chris, and then throw down the hook. I crouch on the runner, one hand holding the handlebar, the other on the hook, as it slides across the surface of the ice. We slide and slide along the river. The hook bounces and skids. Then it hits a log, sticks into it, and stops us dead.

We lurch forward, almost falling over the handlebar. Amazingly, the repair job just creaks with our weight, but holds. The dogs bark, frustrated as they watch the otters slip into a hole in the ice and disappear in the water.

I glance down and freeze.

"Stay still," I say, leaning forward slowly to unclip Bean. "This ice is . . ."

The ice begins to crack under the sled. With both of our weights and all the gear we've packed in the sled, we're far too heavy to be sitting on punky ice.

I feel the cracking through the soles of my muk-luks. I grip the handlebar in horror, unable to move. The ice around us tinkles and creaks like glass.

And then it gives out.

25

I PLUNGE INTO ICY WATER SO COLD, it sucks the wind out of my lungs and I can't catch my breath. My mind is awash in panic. I splash in blind fear. The sound of my wet gulping terrifies me. I sound like I'm drowning.

Finally my chest unclenches, and I can take a long gasp of air. Chris is beside me in the water and

Bean splashes in front of me. I grab his collar and push him up. The ice breaks around his paws. He pushes away from me in panic and in the frothing white of the water, I lose sight of him.

"Bean! BEAN!"

A current is tugging me sideways. The dogs scrabble on the ice against the backwards pull of the sled in the water.

"NO!" I grab the bridle. The gangline is connected to the sled with a covered bungee and two locking carabiners. There's no way I'm going to release it, but I tear at the connections anyway.

"Let it go!" I faintly hear Chris yelling in my ear. The sled is slowly sinking and I'm going with it. I try to clutch the ice with one hand, to keep my head above water. I don't know how to stay afloat without the sled and nothing to grab. But even more terrifying, if it sinks, it will pull the dogs in. I reach farther down and freezing water spills over the top of my anorak. Icy daggers slice into my feet and hands.

"Come on!" Chris tugs on my arm. My hands are like claws. Pretty soon I will have no use of them. I have to get the dogs loose.

"Dorset!" She's the only dog I can see. So precariously close to the thin ice. *Don't fall in.*

"Dorset! Pu — " Water fills my mouth and I gag. Everything below my knees is numb. The pain in my hands is so intense that it feels like they're being sawed off by a million little knives. Hot, sharp knives.

A knife! If I can get to the knife in the back pocket of the sled bag, maybe I could cut the bridle. I reach down into the freezing water but I can't reach while holding the side of the ice. And I can't force my head under. Shameful panic prevents me from doing everything I can to save my dogs.

Chris is yanking on the front of my anorak. I pull away.

"Get out!" Chris screams in my face.

"Sled . . . off . . . too heavy." It's getting harder to

form words. Chris looks into the water and reaches for the sled. He yanks on it, but nothing happens.

"Sled bag." Chris grabs at the Velcro attaching the front of the bag to the sled. It rips away and the front of the bag immediately sinks out of sight. I know it's hanging now from the back stanchions.

Of course, the gear in the bag is what's heavy. We have to get rid of the sled bag so the dogs can pull the sled up. But how are we going to get at the ties in the back? The sled is below the water. I kick at it with feet that are like solid blocks of ice. There's no way I can reach.

"Please!" The only thought I have is of saving the dogs. Visions of my mom back home waiting for me are pushed back. Thoughts of how it must have been for Dad when he was in the river are pushed back, too. *My dogs!* They can't be pulled in. This one goal keeps the terror of being in the water from paralyzing me.

Chris's frantic gaze meets mine. Then he reaches down, ducking half his face under water. He must be reaching for the back stanchions. Will he be able to tear off the sled bag?

His whole head disappears and I stare at the place he went under. My heart explodes with fear. In an instant I feel the release of the weight on the sled and Chris's head pops back up.

Gazoo and Dorset slam into their harnesses, popping their tugs with amazing force. Their nails scratch along the ice surface. The sled starts to move. And then the ice breaks under them and they fall half into the water.

"NO!" *No, no, no, no.*

The bridle digs into my hands as I yank on it to stop the team from being pulled in. I fight the current to push the sled, and fight for air as frigid water splashes around my nose and mouth.

The dogs try to pull the sled up, but it just breaks

more of the ice as it reaches the rim. It needs a boost. I fight to pull myself onto the ice. With my hands sliding, I try to get a hold on the slippery surface, raise up to my chest, then fall back in. I need traction.

Then I remember what is hanging from the handlebar.

When I reach down, my numb hand closes over the familiar shape. I yank my pewter mink from the sled and claw the surface with its pointy tail. It sticks into the ice. Using it like an ice pick, I haul my torso out of the water and the ice holds me. I reach farther above my head for another grip with the ice pick, then hook my other arm around the back stanchion of the sled.

This is it. This has to work.

I haul with every bit of energy I have. I see white with the strain of it.

The wheel dogs pop back onto the ice. The sled slides over the rim. I hang on as if my life depends on it. I know if we don't make it out now, I won't have the strength to try again.

Chris clutches the other stanchion and the sled is pulled along to the solid surface. We slide all the way to the shore. My dogs have done it.

When we get back onto deep snow the drag of Chris and me hanging off the sled stops the team. I pull myself shakily to my knees. The snow hook lies upside down beside the sled and I kick it as I lurch to my feet and stagger toward the dogs. I turn my attention to the trail and trees around us. My gaze darts around, but there's no sign of Bean.

"Come on! W-we have to get moving." Chris is right. If I thought we were in trouble in the water, we're almost guaranteed to die out here now if we don't get warm soon.

"Everything is gone." The sleeping bag, the matches, blankets, the snares, our lunch. We have nothing but the clothes we're wearing. I glance down and see my anorak steaming in the air. White frost is already forming a glaze.

I remember my mom's face when we got the news about Dad. How she spent days locked in her bedroom, not eating. I heard things crashing in there as if they'd been flung against the wall. When she emerged, she was a shell. Ghost white face instead of her normal peach skin. Dull eyes. How would she deal with losing both of us to the river? I think of how I panicked in the water. How all this time I imagined I'd been able to save Dad if I was there. I realize now that I may not have. This belief has been with me for so long, I feel naked without it. I fall onto Blue and he licks my face with a hot tongue.

"G-get up!" Chris commands with a hoarse voice.

My muscles spasm and I jerk as I try to rise. My body is not working right and new terror grips me. I am unable to get up.

Suddenly, my body is being lifted off the ground.

Chris hauls me up in his arms. I clutch at his chest with gnarled hands. He staggers to the sled and falls beside it. I grasp the handlebar and pull myself up. Chris stumbles onto the other runner.

"A-all right," I squeak.

We'll have to back-track along the shore to get to the trail, but the dogs seem to know this and take off in that direction. I almost fall backwards. My clawed hands clutch at the sled. Vicious tremors make it hard to hold on. I've never felt so cold in my life. Not when Dad and I stayed out too late on the trail. Not when I peed my pants from laughing on the sliding hill behind Sarah's, and walked all the way home to hide it. Not even when I was in the river.

Chris shivers beside me. The thin layer of ice that covers us crunches in my ears. I notice with dismay the bare place on the handlebar where Mr. Minky used to be. But he's done his job, almost like Dad knew I'd need him one day. And now he's gone back to the river.

I have to let him go.

We reach the place where we should have crossed the river, and there is nothing but more trail ahead. The same thing we've been looking at for days. Endless spruce dusted with shimmering snow line the path. A shiver grips my body, paralyzes my muscles like a seizure.

Too cold.

I realize that we're not going to make it. We're going to die out here just like Dad did.

The sled hits a bump and we both fall to our knees. I throw myself on the brake to slow the dogs. They stop and look back. Then they lay down on the trail.

Where is Bean? He made it out of the river, didn't he? A pain sears through my heart—it feels as if I'm being flayed from the inside.

"N-need . . . t-t . . . " My teeth chatter so hard, it's a wonder I don't bite off my tongue. Chris tries to get up, then crawls into the sled instead. Without the sled bag, he's able to roll through the upright stan-chion and lay on the bare plastic of the sled bottom.

My body is racked with violent shakes, and hot tears stream down my face. It feels like acid, the way it burns my skin. *Oh, Bean, I'm so sorry.*

26

AT THE THOUGHT OF THE REST of my dogs left out here to die, a stubborn ball of anger shoots through me. I will my arms to obey me and grab the handlebar again. I grind my teeth and concentrate on standing on the runners.

Chris and I have very little time before we both die of hypothermia. Since Dad's accident, I've studied it obsessively. The clock started counting down as soon as we fell in the water. I try to figure out how long that's been. Ten minutes? An hour? Time seems to have both slowed down and sped up.

"All r-right." My voice puffs out like a flame extinguished, but the dogs stand and begin to trot down the trail. They are drained.

I know from my reading that once the shivering stops, my body will start to shut down. I also know it won't hurt, but I can't stop crying.

Through a haze, I see the trail fork ahead. Right or left. Left or right. My mind is slow. I can't think which way to pick, too many decisions. Days and days of bad choices and now I've gone blank with indecision. The wild killed Dad and it's about to kill me, too. I just hope my dogs can somehow make it.

We've stopped again before the fork. I see a shadowy form on the trail. What is that? It looks familiar. It's the wolf! The wolf that had turned around and looked at me that day at the race. He's come to save us!

No, wait. That can't be right. The wolf comes closer. He's limping heavily. My breath catches.

"B–Bean," I croak.

He takes the trail on the right, stops, and looks back at me over his shoulder, then continues on.

"G-g-g." My teeth chatter uncontrollably. I can't form the command, but Blue and Drift follow Bean anyway.

The sled veers to the right and Chris slides on the smooth plastic. He looks up into my eyes. It's as if we're having a silent conversation. His partially singed eyebrows are coated in white. He is a white snowflake, all sparkle and frost.

The sled stops, surprising me back to focus. When I look up, a shot of adrenaline shoots through my brain and my mind clears.

It's our yurt.

I can almost see Dad standing in the doorway smiling at me. "Come on, Icky. What are you doing all wet and cold?"

I shake my head to clear the mirage, but we are still right beside our old yurt. The chimney pipe sticks through the center of the roof and wood is stacked under a tarp next to the door. I stumble off the runners. My leggings are frozen solid, making it almost impossible to walk.

"C-Chris," I croak.

No answer. Chris's head went right under the water. He must be even colder than I am. I have to get us inside.

How is our yurt here? Then I remember it's Cook's now. Are we at Cook's? My thoughts are all jumbled. First, get inside.

I can barely turn the handle to open the door. It takes several tries. Thank you, universe, it's not locked. Finally, I burst through and fall into the middle of the small room. The wood stove sits in the center, and an old smoky smell lingers. A box of kindling is tucked by the door, but besides that the room is empty. My movements are slow, uncoordinated. *Must get warm.*

Chris lies on the sled where I left him. The dogs are already curled up, asleep on the gangline.

"C-Chris, let's g-go."

Chris mumbles and stares at me. I grab his shoulders, but the ice on his jacket is too slippery and I lose my grip. I try again grabbing him under the arms, and hauling backwards. Every muscle in my body strains. He's so heavy, it's impossible.

But then his dead weight shifts. I brace my feet, gather all my strength reserves, and heave. The icy coating over his clothes slides along the ground and we inch over the snow, through the doorway, until we're in the yurt.

Matches. I have to light the fire. I realize I don't have the strength to bring wood in. *Forget the wood, just get the kindling started. You can do this, Vicky.*

Slowly, spastically, I shove kindling into the stove. I see a bag of fire-starter sticks in the kindling box and would smile if my face muscles were working. I stuff the whole bag of starter sticks into the stove, too.

They will help the kindling burn. There's a cast-iron pot on top with a jar of matches inside. Hope flares. My hands are mostly useless. It takes all my effort to grab anything. I manage to get the lid off the jar, but matches spill everywhere.

"N-nargh." I can't form words.

With my body shaking, I crouch over the wooden, planked floor. My fingers won't cooperate—it's as if they belong to someone else. I can't pinch them together hard enough to pick up one tiny match.

I try again.

And again. Tears stream down my cheeks and burn.

NO! We are so close! The warmth is right here, if I can only grab one stupid match.

At last, my fingers grasp several matches at once. It takes fierce concentration to keep them held tightly. I carefully bring my arm down toward the stove. With my heart pounding, I swipe the heads across the surface.

The matches fall.

When I bend again to retrieve them, I tip over and land beside Chris's feet. It's no use.

I crawl up to his head. He's still staring at me with glassy, unfocused eyes.

"Hot," he is saying. "So hot."

I put my head down next to his. I'm hardly shaking any more, but I can't remember why that's bad.

Die. We will die here, in my old yurt, surrounded by my dogs. *The dogs!*

I try to whistle, but no sound comes out. "B–B–Bean!"

I rest my head back down, and then feel hot snuffling in my ear.

Bean.

I turn my face toward him and get stabbed by the frozen tips of his fur. I remember he was in the river with us. The white frost covering his head begins to melt as he stands there, tongue out, grinning at me.

I hear the tinkling of necklines, the ticking of

toenails, as the rest of the team pad inside. They are covered in glistening white slivers. Frosted dogs of ice. My beautiful ice dogs. The sled scrapes across the floor. How did they get the sled in here? They're still attached by the gangline. I reach to unclip Drift, but can't work my fingers.

Bean stands over me and I tap my chest. He immediately steps close, his head bobbing with the effort to use his front leg, and flops down across me. I feel the weight of the rest of the dogs piling on top of me and Chris. Bean licks my face as he leans across my chest. The last thing I hear is the door slamming shut from a gust of wind.

27

THURSDAY

I WAKE UP SHIVERING VIOLENTLY WITH A pain in my fingers and toes so intense, it leaves me gasping. In fact, my whole body hurts. My throat feels like I've eaten a bucket of glass. I open my eyes a slit and look around. It's dark and I can't move. I feel a moment of panic before I realize the hot, damp breath on my cheek is Bean's. My brain takes time to understand I'm on the floor of the yurt under a pile of dogs.

I reach across to Chris and feel him under a mat of steamy, wet fur.

"Chris." I don't recognize the croaking that comes out of my own mouth. My tongue feels swollen.

"Mmmph."

"Chris, are you okay?"

I hear Chris shift. "Ow, oh, ow."

"We found a yurt. The dogs came in. They warmed us up." I notice my clothes are soaking wet now that the ice has thawed. My teeth chatter.

"I love dogs," Chris says.

I slowly climb out from under my fur blanket, wincing as I move. Daggers stab my feet. I think of the pain in the river, and then the freezing after. The absolute cold that had locked my body. My muscles spasm at the memory.

I crawl to the stove and feel around in the dark

for the matches. My fingers close around them and I could cry with relief at how much easier it is to pick them up. Moments later, the darkness of the yurt is lit with the flaring match. The light slices into my eyeballs, but my heart hums with the joy of it. I shove the match into the stove and in an instant, the kindling flares. The heat bounces off my chest.

"Chris, hand me your wet clothes." I shrug off my own heavy anorak, my body still shivering. "I'll lay them out around the stove."

When I peel off my leggings, I notice my underclothes aren't as wet as I thought. The water hadn't seeped in that far. Probably why I'm not dead. But my mukluks feel tight, my feet must be swollen. I'm afraid to think of what they look like. I wiggle my toes and suck in a breath as the pain shoots up my legs. My hands are cracked and swollen like zombie fingers. I can only imagine what my face looks like. But I'm still alive.

We're all alive.

A warm glow from the stove drifts across the

little room. The dogs haven't moved. Whistler sprawls in the center with Gazoo curled up next to her. Dorset is draped across Chris's neck. Amazingly, they're all still attached to the gangline, but stretched out so they didn't tangle. All I can see of Chris is his head sticking up and his arm wrapped around Dorset. When I shuffle out to grab more wood, I rip the tarp covering off and bring it in, too.

"We can wrap ourselves in the tarp until our clothes are dry. It'll help keep the heat in. It's getting warm in here already."

"Where are we? Agh, my feet! And my eyes. My brain is all mushed up. What's a yurt?"

"We're in my old yurt. It's like a round tent, but with a wood platform and wood supports on the walls. Lots of mushers use them. My dad used to set it up in the fall so we had a midway place to go to on our runs. Mom sold it to Cook last year."

I remember how angry I was for that betrayal. But now I could kiss her for it.

"Good, that," Chris says.

The heat on my face seems to wake up my brain. I stick out my aching fingers and hold them toward the stove. It pops and crackles now, spreading a painfully delicious heat through me.

I glance again at the dogs and a rush of emotions threatens to overwhelm me. Relief that everyone is still here with me. Gratitude for their loyalty and body heat, pride that I get to share my life with these amazing animals. My throat aches as I watch Bean's chest rise and fall. He's laying fully stretched out next to Chris's head. When he catches me looking at him he knocks his tail lazily on the floor.

Chris hands me his sopping clothes and this time, I don't even care we're both half naked.

"If Cook set this tent up," I say, "that means we're not far from his yard."

"Where have I heard that before?" But there's a smile in Chris's voice.

"As soon as we get warm, we go. We're almost there, Chris. I know it this time."

We will all surely starve to death here if we don't keep moving. All the food we brought from the trapper's cabin was lost to the river. Now I wish we'd eaten all of the hare right away. Even the dog food is gone. I worry that if I sleep, I may not wake up. We have to make a last effort while we still can.

After I stoke the stove full of wood, I unclip all the dogs, who only move enough to huff at me and then tuck their heads back in. They're so tired, they don't even seem to mind being inside. Bean gives one long, tongue-curling yawn, with a grumble deep in his throat. They're trying to conserve energy. Starving, tired, and only interested in sleep.

With the tarp wrapped around us, and the fire doing its thing, Chris and I slowly warm up. It must be midnight or later by now. Slivers of light from the fire escape out the vents in the stove. Partial light against the black night. It illuminates the dogs with a comforting glow. I lay beside Chris, surrounded by soft, wet breathing, and try to keep my eyes open. As nice as it is to hear my dogs around me, I don't want that to be the last thing I hear.

A deep, predawn darkness stretches across the trail ahead of us. We've been on this trail for what feels like years now. The dogs did not want to go. It was the first time I've ever had to coax them to get up. I wanted to cry at how listless they were, the sparkle in their eyes missing.

I didn't know what to do with Bean. There was no sled bag to put him in, nothing to keep him from sliding around on the plastic sled floor. I thought of trying to hold him somehow, clip him to the handle-bar and make him sit, but in the end, I knew I had to leave him free.

Whistler had lost her booties, but that was a good thing since I wouldn't have been able to take them off for her before they froze on her feet. Gazoo actually looked as if he was going to mutiny when we first got going, tucking his tail down, refusing to move. I gave him extra special attention, stroking his head, whispering in his ear what a handsome, brave dog he is, and I promised him a big steak once we all get home. That seemed to convince him since he's running now. Well, I wouldn't call what we're doing actually running, but we're moving forward.

"I can't see a thing," Chris says beside me.

"That's okay. The dogs can." I'd tell Chris that they can smell the trail, too, feel it under their feet. That they like running at night better than any other time. The dense air pushes the scents closer to the ground. But talking takes too much energy.

I desperately hope that Bean is still on the trail ahead. When we started, he hobbled forward, as if to lead. He should not be running at all. He's limping so heavily, he's going to injure his other shoulder to compensate. This is the worst kind of injury for a sled dog. But I can't carry him. I can hardly hold myself up.

We're obviously on Cook's trails. They're hard packed and wide. We'd be making good time if —

I double over on the runner suddenly, and retch. Nothing comes up, but my stomach twists painfully. I taste bile. My arms, legs, head all feel light. As if they aren't solidly attached. I wipe my mouth and wonder what color my pee is. I can't even remember the last time I peed.

Chris grabs his stomach and retches, too. His outline in the dark is bent over on the runner beside me. A robust sound comes out of him, and I rub his back.

"When's the last time you peed?"

"What?" Chris rubs his face. "You have got to be the strangest—"

"We're dehydrated, Chris. Dangerously dehydrated."

"Oh good, something to add to the list of stuff that's trying to kill us." Chris's voice is rough. He has the look of someone broken. As if he knows we aren't going to make it.

I think about the snow I'd melted in the pot on the stove. How I couldn't get the dogs to drink it. Only Blue licked at it half-heartedly, as if he was just trying to make me happy. They were either too exhausted, or too far dehydrated to want to drink. The few mouthfuls each that Chris and I took wasn't enough. I guess we were too exhausted to drink too.

I pop a handful of snow into my mouth and regret not taking the time to melt more in the pot. The snow trickles down as I hold it on my swollen tongue. My whole life I've known not to eat snow. Dad has told me how it takes my body too much energy to melt it, but I can't help it. I'm so thirsty. And hungry. I feel completely empty.

Chris does the same beside me and I don't say anything. I know we've run out of time. None of this matters. If only I could just sit here for a minute to rest. I've never been so tired.

Pale light seeps through the branches. I see Bean now, lurching ahead on the trail. His head bobs with every step, each one breaking my heart into a million pieces. The rest of the dogs are barely trotting. Even Drift has switched to a lopsided pacing gait. I pedal with a foot, but it's painful. When I stumble, Chris grabs my arm to steady me. The trail climbs a hill, and we both try to waddle beside the sled on ravaged feet. My head pounds. My heart feels as if it's going to explode out my body. My right leg buckles and I fall half on the runner.

The sled stops. I hang my head.

I have nothing left.

Chris crumples beside me and, inexplicably, seeing him give up like that enrages me. I glare at him. "Get up!" My voice is raw, savage.

The dogs sit, watching me over their shoulders. Bean disappears around a corner. A burning need to get them to safety spreads fire through my limbs. I shove at Chris's shoulder, then reach for the handlebar and pull myself up.

"GET UP!" I yell at Chris.

He squints, his chapped lips pulling tight, and climbs slowly to his feet next to me.

"There you are," he says. "Thought I'd lost you."

All of us are barely walking now. No, we're weaving. Staggering up the hill. Every movement is an effort that takes all my will power. I recycle my reasons for moving. One step. Mom. One step. Dogs. One step. Chris. A tiny breeze could tip us over.

And then I see it.

And the dogs hear it. All ears perk at once. Their tails stiffen.

Ahead, dogs begin to howl.

"Is that real?" Chris breathes.

We sag against each other as the team trots toward Cook's yard.

28

MY HEAD FEELS AS IF IT'S been buried in sand. My throat hurts. Breathing hurts. I turn my head and my neck hurts. When I open my eyes, the bright lights stab needles into my retinas. I raise my arm to cover my face, and see tubes coming out of the top of my hand. Then I see my dad's face.

"AUGH!"

Uncle Leonard jumps back as if he's been elec-trocuted. "You trying to give me a heart attack?" He turns his head and shouts, "Sandy, she's awake!"

And now I remember. Cook's. Ambulance. Hospital.

"Stay right here." Uncle Leonard pats my hand, then races out of the room yelling for Mom. As if I'm about to go anywhere.

Finally, Mom appears beside me and takes my hand in her icy ones.

"I'm here." She smiles down at me.

"You . . . you look like a vampire," I manage to say.

She lets out a short laugh, then her white face rearranges and she's bawling. Little blue veins pulse under her bloodshot eyes. Her lids are puffy and red. The normally sleek strands of her hair are hanging in limp strings. Her hand flutters to her red nose and wipes it. She leans down, smoothes my hair off my face. Kisses my forehead.

"And you look like you're grounded. For life."

"Bean! The dogs!" I bolt upright and immediately feel as if I'm going to yak.

"They're fine, Vic. Jeremy Cook took care of them. He even took Bean to the vet. We can't believe you found his yard. You must have done some kind of circular route. He followed your tracks to see you'd crossed at Devil's River."

I hear voices coming from the hall. A moment of panic grips me. *How long have I been here?*

I turn back to Mom. "Is Chris okay? Where is he?"

"You both have some bad frostbite and dehydration, but the doctors say you'll recover. He's in the next room." Mom squeezes my hand. "He's been asking for you, too."

She looks down at me and her eyes start to tear up again. We both talk at once.

"Mom, I'm sorry I went without telling you."

"I'm sorry I didn't take you to Cook's."

Mom suddenly lunges at me and wraps me in her arms. "Vic, Vic, Vic," she chants, rocking me.

"Mom, too tight, Mom!"

We laugh and she wipes her nose, then holds me at arm's length. "You are so stubborn. But I heard from Chris all you did. How you found him and saved him and I'm so proud of you. So proud." She rubs my arm. "Your dad . . . would be so proud of you, too."

"Mom," I rush to get this out before the knot in my throat completely prevents me from talking. "I know it wasn't your fault. And it wasn't my fault. Sometimes stuff just happens that you can't control."

Her hands go to her mouth and she nods, tears spilling from her eyes.

"But I really, really, really want to stay in Alaska. And run dogs, Mom. I want to hear wolves, and maybe learn guitar, and start going to parties. Maybe we should have a party."

I feel as if I've just let go of something heavy. Like I could float off this bed right now.

Mom leans down and hugs me. "Baby, we're not going anywhere. I love living in Alaska, too. This is home. This is everything you live for, I know that. And I know that I haven't been a good mom since losing Dad." Her face looks pained as she continues. "Vicky, I'm sorry I belittled your relationship with your dad that day. I know you relied on each other out there. I didn't mean what I said, and I should've said this sooner. But now we should promise each other something." She looks me in the eye. "We shouldn't try to deal with things on our own, okay? We've still got each other, let's not forget that." Her last words squeak out, and then she starts to bawl, which gets me started and we're both hiccupping and blubbering when Uncle Leonard walks in.

"You sure know how to get attention, kiddo," he says. His stride is so much like Dad's long, purposeful stride. "Search-and-rescue crews, game wardens. You've been on the local news every night."

Mom wipes her eyes and looks from me to Uncle

Leonard. "I'm just going to talk to the doctors down the hall, Vic. I'll be right back." She stands tall, smoothing her hands down the front of her shirt in a gesture that is so familiar, I'm almost overwhelmed again.

I twist around and wrestle down the metal arm of the hospital bed. Uncle Leonard helps me as I swing my legs over the side. My feet are wrapped.

"Looks like you have some mending to do before the White Wolf." Uncle Leonard gives me a playful punch on the arm that actually hurts.

"Hey! I almost died of frostbite, remember?" I rub my arm.

He laughs and then his face changes. In a blink, it goes from his normal smile to something strained with anguish. His bright eyes swim and he clutches me in a tight embrace.

"I'm so glad you're safe. I don't know what I'd do if I lost you, too."

I wrap my arms around his middle, careful with the IV tubes, and hold on as my own throat closes.

"I miss him so much, kiddo. So much."

We separate, and Uncle Leonard pats my shoulder awkwardly. Now that I look for it, I see within his face the strain of grief. I see that he feels compelled to be the one to watch over me for Dad.

I take his hand. "We have to watch over each other, Uncle Leonard. I learned that at least on my little trip."

His Adam's apple bounces as he looks at me with a new, open expression. He nods and gently takes my head under his arm to rub his knuckles across the top of my head.

"Augh, stop that!"

"Far as I know, no frostbite up here."

The ride home is a blur of telephone poles and speeding vehicles. We seem to be traveling at an insane pace compared to what I'd been used to for the last week. I grip the handle above the truck door and try to relax. It's strange to think that the whole time I was gone, the rest of the world continued on. As if there was no race for survival going on just on the other side of those trees. Cars still zoomed around carrying people who went to work, to school, got their cavities filled, traveled in a girl-pack to go to the bathroom, turned in their science projects.

I feel as if I've just stepped out of an alternate universe where I've been for the last ten years, and all time here had stopped until I got back on. I've changed, but the rest of the world hasn't.

Mom grips my hand with one of hers as she steers with the other. It hurts my fingers but I don't want her to stop.

"Here we are," she says. "Home at last. You'd better start calling people, Sarah first. But the whole town has been holding vigil."

We pull into our driveway and the dogs start a chorus of welcome. My heart trips and I fling open the door before we've rolled to a stop.

"Careful . . . " Mom is saying, but I don't catch

the rest as I jump out. I want to sprint to the dog yard, but landing on my feet quickly reminds me of my last few days. I end up hobbling awkwardly, gritting my teeth, my heart racing with happiness. Tears erupt out of me when I see Bean matching my hobble as he moves around his circle.

All the dogs greet me as if it's been months since they've seen me. But they do that even after I leave for ten minutes. Still, it fills my soul to see them all, including the ones that didn't come along on our adventure. Even Beetle seems insanely happy I'm home. I bury my fingers in their coats, smell their doggy breath, and feel a rush of joy so intense, it burns behind my eyes.

As I limp around with the shovel, cleaning the yard, I make a promise to myself. I will always enjoy doing dog chores this much. I won't ever take my life for granted.

29

FRIDAY

THE NEXT MORNING I SPEND TIME with each of the dogs separately, feeding them beaver steaks that Uncle Leonard bought from Mr. Oleson. I talked to the vet last night and today I have to break the news to Bean that his racing days are most likely over. With deep tissue injuries in both shoulders, he has a weakness now that I can't let him strain. Even just tripping on one moose track punched in the trail could cause more damage that I'm not willing to risk. No, we're going to go for slow, fun runs and then try massage, compress wraps, glucosamine, and whatever else I can do to keep the arthritis at bay. I won't stop him running though. Not running at all would kill his spirit.

"I'm so sorry, Beanie. But retirement won't be that bad." He looks at me with knowing eyes.

"Who wants to win races anyway?"

I stroke Bean's chest as he sits in front of me, a wide-mouthed goofy grin across his face. We've sat like this so many times. But this time, I really see him. Like he sees me. His gaze is steady, burning into me with the intensity of our bond.

Racing is just an excuse to spend time with the dogs out on the trail, doing what they love. How could I have forgotten that? Still, before our next race, Bean is going to have to help me train Drift to be a better leader. We don't need any side trips in the middle of a race.

"We're going to go as slow as you need to, chum. But after we've had some rest, okay?" I hold up a fat chunk of beaver meat. "For now, do you have any interest in this?"

Baked corn bread, roasting moose, and bubbling brown gravy odors waft out of the kitchen along with a cranked Johnny Cash tune. Mom sings off-key. I don't even turn on Timbaland to drown out the noise that Mom calls music. It's just good to hear Mom sound so happy.

Sarah is the first to arrive with her entire family. She's wearing an off-the-shoulder, low-cut shirt with a black lace push-up bra underneath. And the black lace is sort of the first thing you see. Her tight mini is paired with hot pink leg coverings that reach halfway up her thighs. As she's coming in for a hug, I point.

"What the heck are those?"

"This is going to be the latest rage, Vic! Leg

warmers are coming back to fashion. Cripes, you've been gone for days and you're *so* behind!"

She laughs and a delicate little snort sneaks out and I'm so delighted to hear that sound again, my eyes start to well up. Her eyes well up too, and we hug with a fierceness that surprises me. We rock back and forth. Her familiar vanilla body lotion scent brings on more tears. I'm going to have to get a grip or this will be a long night.

"Oh, Vicky." She touches the frostbite still visible on my nose and cheeks. "I was so freaking out. Freakin' drama. But I should have known you'd find a way back, and save a stray while you were doing it." She dabs at her eyes and looks behind me. "I've seen his picture on the news. I want to see if he's that cute in person. Where is he? Is he here? Point him out."

"Uh, not here, not cute, definitely not your type."

"Oooh! Liar. I'm intrigued——"

"There you are, Victoria. Oh Lord, I'm so

relieved you made it back." Mrs. Wicker, my old youth group leader and owner of the feed store in town, steps close and gives me a quick, perfumed hug.

Sarah whispers as she walks away, "I want full details later."

"You'd think that those fellows that were searching would have been able to find you," Mrs. Wicker is saying.

"We saw them," I tell her. "One of the helicopters. But I think we were hard to spot."

"Well, they should be better trained. Lord, how could they miss you?"

"It's okay, Mrs. Wicker. We made it back without them."

"Yes! That's the main thing. You're home and that boy you found is back safe, too." She lowers her voice and continues in a scandalous hush. "They're from Canada, you know. His poor mother here all alone without a man. She's a single mom, you know. Terrible business. And then losing her only son just after they arrive. Oh Lord, can you imagine it? I nearly break out in hives just thinking of it!"

I nod. There's no stopping Mrs. Wicker when she's on a roll, so I don't even try. She fans her face, then leans in again.

"But she's never seen such a helping and caring community as us. Someone was always over there keeping her company. Bringing casseroles and making tea." Her voice gets louder and faster with each word.

When she says this it brings a hazy memory of everyone coming to our house last year. Bringing food for Mom and me, too. I feel a sudden tenderness toward Mrs. Wicker, then realize she's still talking so try to focus.

" . . . She's most grateful to you, Victoria. You'll probably get a medal for saving him, you know. Oh Lord, can you imagine, our own Victoria Secord, a national hero!" She's practically shouting in my ear now.

"That reminds me, I wanted to invite her to a welcome party at my house next Saturday. You and your mother will have to come too, dear. The whole community is invited."

"That sounds great—"

"Lord, listen to me! We're all just so happy you're *alive*. Don't worry about your next dog food shipment, dear. Mr. Wicker and I plan to have a pallet delivered to you *free of charge*. Our little way of saying how proud we are of you." Her whole body fluffs up like a preening bird.

"Wow! Thank you so much, Mrs. Wicker. I—"

"Yes—not a *full* pallet you understand. One or two bags. It's nothing. Now you rest up." She beams, adjusts the fabric over her bosom, then hurries away, presumably on a mission to find Chris's mom.

Most everyone from my class is here, along with their families. Mr. Oleson, Mr. Wicker, the Cooks, all the members from search-and-rescue. The hugs and tears, laughter, and screeches of welcome make the time fly by. But then the food is spread out and I stare at the mounds of it—all just sitting there.

It's beautiful.

When I dig in, though, I realize my stomach must have shrunk, because I can only eat one bite of a few things. But the real food— solid, delicious, hot— nearly brings more tears to my eyes. If everyone could almost die, the world would be a happier, more thankful place.

"Are you going to finish that?" a familiar voice says next to me.

I whirl around. "Back off, man, get your own. How's your pit with the spears working out? Getting any meat?"

Chris's pale face is as ravaged as mine, with red blotches, and white, waxy-looking spots across his nose and cheeks.

"You look awful," he says, then grins and looks like Chris.

"Yes, well, on you—it's sort of an improvement."

We both smile, and stand there knowing we share something that no one else will ever truly understand.

"So, I wondered if I could like, borrow one of those dog coats."

I give him a questioning look.

"To use as a pattern. I want to make something for the dogs. And I was thinking a sign for your sled bag for your next race that says, 'Chris is awesome.'"

I cross my arms and try not to laugh.

"'Chris is a bit awesome'?" He raises his brows. "No? At least can I keep the pink tights?"

I give in and laugh, then grab his hand. "There's someone I want you to meet."

We weave our way into the living room to a place that I have avoided for more than a year. I turn my attention to a photo in a large black frame hanging on the wall.

"That's my dad."

Chris studies the picture as I soak in the image of my dad smiling, wearing his soft-worn flannel shirt that he insisted on, even for a professional photo session. His arm is around Mom, his hand on my shoulder. The permanent sun creases are around his eyes, standing out on his tanned face and making his gaze seem as if he's looking right at me. I stare right back and know I'll never stop missing him. That won't ever go away.

"I see where you get your hair. Where does the stubborn come from, Mom or Dad?"

Dad used to say people come into our lives for a reason. I give Chris's hand a squeeze. Mandolin music reaches us from the kitchen. Chris's teasing expression turns into a question.

"Mom," I say. "She's a good mandolin player."

The music is joined by hand clapping and stomping. Suddenly, standing in my living room surrounded by everyone, I feel like Mom and I are a family again. A chorus of howls comes up from the dog yard and joins with the music in the kitchen. My dogs sound happy.